EVEN A NOISE THAT SOFT FELT WRONG in that place. But when they didn't answer, I took a few steps forward to inspect the Darquets. They were all female, and the fungus covered their bodies in the same strange patterns I'd noted on the earthen walls. The pulsing lights moved from the walls and across the floor—earning a startled squeak from me as it ran under my feet—and spiraled up the bodies of the three Darquets.

The light pulsed three times then, on the third pulse, pooled in their eyes. That was a little creepy. The Darquets turned and stared at me. *Yup, now it's a horror show. Great.*

I backed up, and the Darquet nearest me turned and stepped off the platform, fungus clinging to her like strands of silk.

"You shall be judged," she said in a voice as cold as ice. She raised a hand, and the fungus erupted from her fingertips like a spider shooting out its webbing. Before I could scream or run or faint, the fungus coated my body, winding its way up over my skin until it settled around my mouth. I bit down hard on the inside of my lips and tried to twist away, but the fungus shifted and moved up through my nostrils and down through my ears.

The heroine in a story would've let out a full-on bloodcurdling scream right then. But I couldn't.

THE THREE-FOLD SUNS

The Rapscallion
Project Clear Sight
The Diplomats of Dar

THE DIPLOMATS OF DAR

THE THREE-FOLD SUNS

Book 3

by

ELIZABETH KNOLLSTON

LEWIS BROS PRESS

Copyright © 2023 Elizabeth Knollston

The Diplomats of Dar
The Three-Fold Suns Book 3
All Rights Reserved

This book, or parts thereof, may not be reproduced in any form without permission.

This is a work of fiction. All characters and events in this book are fictitious. Any similarity to real persons, living or dead, is coincidental and not intended by the author.

ISBN Paperback: 978-1-959159-05-6
ISBN Ebook: 978-1-959159-06-3

Cover Art and Interior Design © Elizabeth Knollston
Editing by Red Adept Editing Services

Published by Lewis Bros. Press
PO Box 261
Larned, KS 67550

www.elizabethknollston.com

*for Naomi
and all of the encouragement,
advice, and found family
without you, these books
wouldn't have become reality*

1

Schooling Time

I worked my way through the labyrinth of corridors onboard the *Samaritan*, munching on an old-fashioned egg-and-sausage biscuit—with a twist. I was taking full advantage of Miles's cooks, who'd topped the egg with a bit of poached quili, which gave the sandwich a delicate hint of spice. A bit of comfort food never hurt anyone when they're the center of unwanted attention.

Despite the horrific development of learning about the depravity of my brother, along with the chaos resulting from his destruction of Lunar 5, I'd stuck with my decision to throw Miles into the brig. Each morning since that decision, I made my way to Central Processing and asked Miles about the smart-bots he'd infected me with and why he'd thrown me to the mercy of the Star Eaters. For the first few days, Miles laughed, joked, and lounged around as though he didn't have a care in the world. He would flash me his cryptic smile as he casually leaned against the wall and stated I wasn't ready for those answers.

Right.

As if being held captive—twice—being injected with multiple substances, learning that my brother was as messed up as the other crazies I'd had the misfortune of getting to know, and being forced to watch Cain's torture wasn't enough to make me "ready" for whatever mysterious revelations the universe had in store for me.

As I made my way through the corridors, I passed one of the crew, who gave me a respectful nod and said, "Captain."

I'd been tempted to relinquish my command of the *Samaritan* to Commander Lio, an individual of mixed Telt and human ancestry, who had a quiet yet authoritative air about him. But maintaining my connection to the *Samaritan*'s artificial intelligence core, Sam, meant I controlled Central Processing. Miles couldn't bribe or threaten anyone on the ship to release him.

I really wasn't the captain and felt a little embarrassed each time the crew acknowledged my title on the ship. I had the sneaking suspicion the crew wasn't recognizing me just because I held the highest level of authority within the Sam network, but that there was also a touch of genuine respect in their salutes and salutations. After the complete debacle with the InterGalactic Justice System on the *Justus*, the crew credited me with their escape—with Sam's help, of course.

In reality, Commander Lio was in control. We'd come to a mutual agreement, using a surprisingly small number of words. I also suspected Lio wasn't a big fan of Miles and enjoyed seeing his employer forced to sulk. I would have to admit I enjoyed it as well.

That time, before I headed off for round eight—or

nine, I'm not sure anymore—with Miles, I stopped by the lab and checked in with Dr. Ashter. While the renowned xenologist might not have held much respect for my father—the infamous Wats Hawking Orion, convicted traitor against humanity and a man I realized I'd never known—Dr. Ashter seemed to hold a small spark of respect for me.

He'd also been forthcoming with me, teaching me as though I'd signed up for a private Star Eater 101 course for little old me.

"Morning, Doc. Any updates?" I asked as I popped the last of the breakfast sandwich into my mouth and stopped next to a large holo platform.

Every time I'd stopped and chatted with him, a holo of a planet was slowly rotating in the center of the room, a clue to his current focus. The platform was dark that day—not a good sign.

The xenologist turned and shook his head. "No, I'm afraid not."

Dr. Ashter had spent a fair amount of credits on life extensions. Biologically, the man was in his nineties, but physically, he appeared to be in his thirties, maybe even late twenties. Except that day, his skin looked sallow, with a few wrinkles around his mouth and eyes.

"Doc, you feeling okay?"

He waved a hand to dismiss my concern. "Review. Timeline."

Ever the professor.

"The Star Eater cult is a phenomenon known for centuries, with limited sightings on multiple worlds. Rare enough to warrant only limited or academic curiosity as the cult kept to the shadows and existed in rumors and popular back-alley myths. But approximately two years after the beginning of the Cricade Wars, Star Eater activity spiked with an unprecedented number of sightings.

"Numerous cult members were first spotted on Mandarian's Rhine with a slew of subsequent reports across multiple locations. This broke with traditional patterns. The media quickly ran the stories, but despite journalistic, academic, and the few oddball inquires, no one could pin the Star Eater cult to one species. Or provide any reasonable idea as to their motivation. Self-proclaimed members of the cult were known only by the tightly woven blue robes they wore and their staunch refusal to answer questions. Because of the number of deaths surrounding Star Eater activity, the cult rapidly became a symbol of fear," I recited like the good little parrot I was.

I could be a walking encyclopedia when I wanted to be. <*Take that,*> I silently thought and waited, expecting to hear a response. Despite what Dr. Ashter and the chief medical officer, Dr. Kell, had informed me, I expected the telepathic connection between Cain and me to be fully restored at any moment.

I got nothing back. But that didn't mean it wasn't going to happen. Sam provided regular updates as well, and each time her report came in, I crossed my fingers and hoped for good news.

Cain had talked me down from killing Commandant Yilmaz after her unwelcome hospitality on board the *Justus*. I suppose I was in denial, not wanting to believe what Dr. Kell repeatedly told me concerning the extensive amount of neurological damage Cain had sustained, damage he'd gotten because he reached out to help me when I'd been teetering on the edge. I was working hard not to dwell on that.

Cain will be fine. The ornery man will wake up, and everything will go back to how it'd been. But deep down, I feared that wasn't true. Nothing could go back to the way it'd been—not my life nor my short-lived time with Cain. We'd both sustained too much emotional and physical damage to be who we had been.

"And?" Dr. Ashter asked, pushing me out of my melancholy thoughts.

The tone of his voice was stern, and I had an inkling that any first-year students taking one of his classes would crawl into a hole after their first day and sob uncontrollably.

"Star Eater activity has been sighted on the known worlds, including the Glipglow home world, the Telt home world, Kibol 3, Selarious, Epo-5, and Dar," I said.

Dr. Ashter raised an eyebrow.

"Most are worlds my father worked on, plus a few he hadn't made it to," I said. I'd made the connection the previous night after reading through the latest group of reports Dr. Ashter had provided. The realization was a shock, yet it also wasn't, somehow.

I mean, mix up the unexpected aid from the Star Eaters when Mrs. Gol had toyed with me on the *Rapscallion*, and add the communication the cult had had with my father as evidenced by what my lawyers told me, and I wasn't really surprised when the dots connected.

As wonky as that connect-the-dots puzzle might have been, it was finally all coming together. It's like when someone buys a Rizzly art piece. They stick it up on the wall then turn it one way and the other, trying to figure out which way is up.

Dr. Ashter nodded and walked over to me. "Your father petitioned to work on Dar." He asked no question in there, merely making a statement of fact. He activated the hologram. "But they denied him access."

Then I nodded. "Yup. I remember that. He wasn't happy, moped around for weeks after receiving the final verdict. I think it really surprised him the Ruling Council denied him access."

"It wasn't the Council that decided," Dr. Ashter said, as calm as a ship tethered to a space dock.

I turned and stared at him. "What?"

With a heavy sigh, Dr. Ashter moved to the opposite side of the platform, but his gaze remained fixed on the holo. "The Ruling Council alerted me to Wats's petition and asked me for my thoughts on the matter. They knew his reputation, as did most academics—methodical, expedient, and most thorough, by all accounts an acceptable person to allow access to Dar. But"—he lifted his eyes to look at me—"I knew something about Wats few did. I knew what he was really after."

"Star Eaters," I sighed. "You don't think you could have just led with all of this? Instead of waiting for me to play catch-up?"

"I wasn't sure of your motivations," Dr. Ashter replied.

"And now? Have you decided whether I'm going to

take over the known worlds as some evil flaming ball of melting metal?" I asked, and if you don't get the reference, look up the heavy metal rock band, Flaming Fuel.

"No, I don't believe you're destined to be a fiery goddess. I believe your motivations are pure."

My mouth dropped open. I wouldn't have expected someone with his reputation to know about Flaming Fuel. Will wonders never cease?

I should've felt annoyed at Dr. Ashter making me work for the information instead of saving time and just coming out and telling me, but Dr. Ashter was playing true to who he was, an academic, and despite the drawn-out way he was providing answers, at least he was doing so.

I snapped my mouth shut and grinned. "Good. No fiery balls of doom in my future, then. But…" I had to ask, "So you were the reason he was turned away?"

My correct assumption earned the merest hint of a smile. "Yes. I wasn't entirely sure of his motivations, but I knew whatever they were, it wasn't in the best interest of Dar."

"Why?"

"Do you know who your father worked for?" Dr. Ashter asked.

I was sorely tempted to roll my eyes, but I answered. "Various companies, corporations. Whoever needed that type of work done could hire him out. He wasn't ever tied to a particular schooling branch."

"No, he wasn't. But his employers weren't random or multiple. Wats worked for one corporation, the one who funded his schooling and the one that wanted to bribe his way onto the Exploration and Historical Research Panel."

"Wait, let me guess," I interrupted. "A corporation that somehow ties back to Mrs. Gol, right?"

Dr. Ashter nodded. "Among a wide selection of other wealthy and powerful individuals. Yes."

"And the corporation is?"

"ChowHo Insurance," Dr. Ashter stated.

I laughed. "You're kidding me." But when his expression didn't change, I stopped laughing. "You're not joking, are you?"

He shook his head.

That made a certain amount of sense in the whole messed-up direction my life had taken. An insurance company was always in demand and could gain access to just about anything they wanted, with the right paperwork and attitude. Wow. I would have lost the ship if I'd made a bet on that.

"Research the company. ChowHo has its legitimate branches, but read between the lines. See what you can find," Dr. Ashter said.

I'd learned a lesson from previous conversations and knew I wasn't going to get much more out of him. The man had given me an assignment, and once I'd come up with an answer, he would talk again.

He turned back to what he'd been working on, and I stared at the holo of Dar. What could Dar have to do with the Star Eaters? As far as I could tell, the Ruling Council had never added their voice to the growing alarm at the ever-increasingly violent actions of the cult. And honestly, Dar culture didn't give off a hint that they would want anything to do with a group like the Star Eaters. I'm not trying to be snooty or anything—that's just their vibe.

I desperately wished Cain was awake so that I could discuss that with him. To my distaste, the next best person for hashing out a few theories was Miles. But talking with the would-be emperor of Old Earth was like trying to herd a roving group of feral grav-cats.

I left the lab with some torturous thoughts on my mind—as in methods for torturing Miles into giving me the answers I wanted. There had to be a way to make the man tell me something useful.

"Excuse me, Captain?" A young crewman rushed up to me. "I apologize for the interruption, but you've got an incoming message. Private comms only and marked urgent."

"Thank you."

I headed for the nearest communications node. A plethora were scattered throughout the *Samaritan*, and I found one tucked away in a corner not too far from the lab. I stepped up into the alcove and activated the privacy screen.

"Mahia Orion," I said.

The node's interface flared to life, and I heard Sam's voice.

"Please state your request."

"I've got a message in the queue."

"Incoming message for Mahia Eimariana Orion, private comms. Please hold still while the system confirms."

Sam scanned my face and pinged the HalfLife biochip. I had no need for false digital fingerprints anymore

and had asked Sam to scrub my HalfLife chip clean.
"Identity confirmed. Proceed?"

"Yes."

The node opened like a flower hocked up on stims to reveal a screen embedded underneath. Standard disclaimers scrolled by, and once through the red tape rigmarole, I could see who'd sent the message.

Urgent
From Master of Dentar
Message on a seventeen-hour delay
Reply needed immediately

2

Messages Galore

I breathed a sigh of relief. After having Miles locked up in the brig, I'd sent a message to the master. I figured that if Miles wasn't going to provide answers about the sneaky smart-bots he'd infected me with, then I knew someone out there who could. Who better than a master Glipglow?

Dr. Kell hadn't been offended when I told her what I needed. She monitored my vital signs, but the smart-bots were beyond her scope of expertise. So she assisted me in my endeavor by taking blood samples, processing them through the medical system's computer, and doing a whole host of other medical tests. Despite my not being able to provide the master with an actual smart-bot, at least he could examine my physiological data to put together a profile of what I might be dealing with.

I opened the message and read.

Send rendezvous coordinates at once.

And that was it.

"Sam, where's the rest of the message?"

"Please state the malfunction."

I bit my tongue. If I'd been in charge of coding the ship's help desk persona, believe you me, things would've been a tad bit different. But fine. "The message hasn't been displayed in its entirety. Please reload and display the message."

After a few seconds' delay, the first screen appeared with the standard disclaimers. I flicked through it and was returned to the one line.

Send rendezvous coordinates at once.

"Is that really it?" I asked. I'd sent him piles of data to sift through and had been confident the master would provide me with some kind of clarity regarding what Miles had done to me. To be fair to Miles, though, I was fairly sure my strange visions—hallucinations, I'm not sure what to call them—weren't Miles's doing but the Star Eaters'. One of those supposed options Miles had mentioned.

But while Dr. Kell had been diligent in keeping up to date with my exams, as far as she could see, I was perfectly healthy, minus the smart-bots, of course, and the fact they seemed to have migrated to my spinal column. All my scans showed no evidence of neurological damage or anything suspect that might have explained what'd been happening.

To be honest, I hadn't told Dr. Kell about the visions. I wanted to have some kind of handle on what might've been going on before I delved into the world of wacky hallucinogenic lights.

What a bucket of pickled eels.

Pardon my language. I've watched a tad bit too many

Neetho holodramas to take my mind off of everything late at night.

With the one-sentence message staring up at me, I opened a reply channel and stared at the screen. Where could I rendezvous with the master? We were on route to Dar, and the route from where Lunar 5 used to be to Darquet-controlled space didn't have a lot of stops along the way. And I wasn't interested in making a detour. Cain needed help.

I supposed my answers were going to have to wait. For the time being. *Unable to rendezvous at this time. Will send coordinates for a meetup at a later date. Please send what information you can.*

My finger hovered over the send icon. I hated to be so vague with the master, but even with heavy encryptions, all communications were heavily monitored, no doubt. Not just because a certain commandant of the IGJ threatened to come after me—she was like a dog with a bone—but security systems had to be on high alert after Lucas's little show and tell.

Then again, anyone with half a brain should've been able to figure out where the *Samaritan* was headed. First, every kid who's gone through Intro to Ships, Designs, and Emergencies—a course required throughout the known worlds—could extrapolate our course trajectory. And second, if they'd been following my little saga, they would know I wasn't going to sit back and do nothing to help Cain. So that meant I was in a race against the known worlds. Would I be able to get Cain the help he needed before someone caught up to us?

So be it. Life was what life was right then. I sent the message.

"Do you wish to play your other messages?" Sam asked.

"What?"

"You have seventy-nine messages in the queue. Do you want them displayed?"

I stood up a little straighter. "Why wasn't I notified about them?" The system should have pinged me when they arrived.

"All notifications have been placed on silent. Please state the command to reactivate notifications."

Rotten jellyfish, I'd forgotten. When we took the *Samaritan* back from the IGJ, the link I'd set up with the Sam network had been inundated with notifications: repair lists, crew requests, damage reports, a catalog list of injuries, and the list of the dead. It'd been too much. That was when Commander Lio and I'd come to an agreement, and I'd silenced the notifications.

Whoops.

"Reactivate notifications for all incoming messages addressed to me."

"Notification request processed."

"Thanks. Display my messages, please. All of them."

The screen blinked then rolled through the list. Requests from various media outlets for interviews were there, no doubt because of my brother boldly claiming responsibility for destroying an entire lunar base and once again splashing the Orion name in the news. And a handful of hate messages had come in. I'd learned to ignore those pretty quickly after my father was arrested.

The light ping of a bell went off in my head, followed by an update from Sam: *[Notification alert. Incoming message from Wonderlust Media. Interview Request.]*

A second ping. *[Notification alert. Incoming message with blocked coding. You and your family should never have been—]*

"Block that one," I quickly instructed.

[Message blocked.]

I turned my attention back to the screen. *I need to look at what my—*

Ping. *[Notification alert. Incoming message from Hart Thorgo. Go to—]*

"Block it," I snapped. "Screen incoming messages. Send alerts for messages from my contact list only." Granted, that was a rather small list. I could count my contacts on two hands, but give me a break, people.

"Request processed."

Now. To the messages from my lawyers.

I started with the oldest and worked my way up to the most recent—no surprises there. The offices of Strobe & Bloodhearst had informed me of the IGJ seizure of the letter Commandant Yilmaz had shown me, along with a laundry list of agreements I'd signed off on initially, stating they weren't to be held responsible and blah blah blah.

Three other messages repeated the same information, then the next was an apology from a Cleary Station clerk. I hadn't expected that. I tried to compose a reply but didn't know what to write. *Sorry my messed-up life got you sucked up into the crazy land of the IGJ.* Or perhaps *No worries. It happens.*

I moved on. The latest message from my lawyers opened, and I frowned. "Sam, rerun the message. It looks like the trace-back coding got scrambled."

"Processing request."

Mixed-up coding wasn't an anomaly even though tech companies did their best to ensure it rarely happened. But with sending messages across the known worlds, tying into multiple receivers with jumbled-up tech from a slew of different species and the distances the messages traveled—well, accidents were bound to happen.

"There appears to be a large data packet embedded within the trace-back coding. Permission to retrieve?"

Alright. So perhaps that wasn't an accident. "Yes."

"The process will take an unspecified amount of time."

"Notify me when you're finished," I instructed Sam.

Then I scrolled through the messages one more time to make sure I hadn't missed anything, and when I decided I hadn't, I deleted most of them.

I stepped out of the alcove, wondering what my lawyers had tried to send. Maybe it hadn't really been a message from them. It was hard to tell anymore. My thoughts drifted to the one place I didn't want them to go—Lucas. He was a major reason I was binging Neetho holodramas late at night. Every time I closed my eyes, I pictured Cain in medical, Miles standing off in the corner, gleefully chuckling, and my brother with a wry smile on his lips with an unpleasant look in his eyes while he loomed over me. Lucas had never hurt me as a kid, but some of his scheming had been extremely unpleasant. I'd always chalked it up to a kid rebelling against his father, upset at being yanked from place to place without the time to put down any roots.

But having looked back on several of our misadventures, I was questioning what I'd really known about Lucas. Had our father known about the little vicious streak running through his son? I shuddered. I really hoped not because, if he had, then he shouldn't have let Lucas leave as he did.

I didn't know where to even start tackling the issues my brother brought up—not just with Lunar 5, but with his message. I wondered if he was watching me. That would've been pretty creepy, if you ask me. But he'd known what was going on by referencing Cain and Yilmaz. While I didn't relish hashing out family history with people, that had been something I'd talked with Lio about. Maybe we had a spy on board the *Samaritan*. Lio assured me we didn't. Then I pointed out the two IGJ agents who'd helped capture the ship, and Lio had leaned forward and very quietly said, "It has been seen to."

Also, I knew Lio and the command officers were tackling the larger issues of the origin of the tech Lucas had used—maybe the Jumjul or a species who'd been quietly working on it in the dark or humanity. No one knew for sure. No one was owning up to it except Lucas. Everyone was scrambling to find a way to protect themselves.

Miles might've known, but I didn't want to distract the would-be emperor from the one task he needed to accomplish.

Lucas had said he would be there for me when I was ready. But I didn't know why he thought I would go to him, especially after what he'd done, not to mention flaunting that damned sun tattoo. I wondered if he'd followed in our father's footsteps or known Mrs. Gol.

If he had, then I couldn't bring myself to acknowledge that implication—not yet. I was still processing what I'd learned about Pops. While I was getting better at acknowledging that reality, I wasn't ready to tackle round two.

After I get Cain fixed up, then we go down that particularly nasty rabbit hole.

3

Down the Research Rabbit Hole

I dismissed the guard on duty at the block of cells Miles was assigned to at Central Processing. That wasn't a big deal as Miles was the only one currently there.

"I'm a bit peckish," Miles quipped as I came into view.

"Too bad you missed out on breakfast. The chef whipped up some fabulous eggs with poached quili," I said.

"From my reserved stock?" Miles asked.

I nodded. "You betcha."

He squinted his eyes and huffed. "You'd better have plans to restock my stores when I'm out of here."

I shrugged. "Who says I'm planning on letting you out? Maybe you'll just rot in this place. I'm confident we can find other charges that will stick. You're not exactly a squeaky-clean specimen of honor and valor, now, are you?"

Miles leaped off the poor excuse for a cot and charged to the edge of his holding cell. "You've got no idea what I am," he snarled.

"I would've thought you would have more stamina than this. You're barely past a week in the brig, and you're what? Stir-crazy? Not enjoying rationed food?"

His fury vanished as he cocked a leg, placed a hand on his hip, and twirled the other in the air. "It has a tendency to bring the worst out in me, I'm afraid. Spending time in the dank, dark dungeons of Old Earth can have that lasting effect."

I raised an eyebrow. *That was a tidbit I didn't know.* "Fascinating, but as much as I would enjoy learning your excruciatingly dull history, I'm much more interested in what you can tell me about the smart-bots. You remember those pesky little critters you injected me with?"

Miles shook his head. "Mahia, my dear. What have I told you? You're simply—"

I snarled. "Enough of that foggy jargon, you little scuttle crab." Again, too many Neetho holodramas. "It's time you coughed up some helpful information."

"Scuttle crab?" Miles asked then doubled over in laughter. "I haven't heard that expression since... Well, I don't know. But somehow, I like it."

Of course the madman would like it. "Miles, come on. Isn't this getting tedious?"

He wiped away a few tears and shook his head. "Perhaps. But there is a time for everything. One of the hardest lessons I've had to learn." He paused and grew thoughtful. "If you really feel as if you need a peek behind the veil, then might I suggest you visit Deck

Fifteen? The rec hall? It might surprise you what you find on board a ship such as this."

"Right. Fine. At least Dr. Ashter has been helpful," I muttered.

"Really?" Miles asked with a glint in his eye that I didn't like. "And what, pray tell, has he been telling you?"

I grinned. "You're not ready for that kind of information. Sorry."

Miles pursed his lips and studied me. "Not every helping hand is what it appears to be."

"And what's that supposed to mean? Are you jealous? That I'm working with someone else and not playing along with your game? Is that it? For crying out loud," I huffed, "you're the one who hired him. He's doing what you employed him to do."

When Miles didn't answer, I shook my head. "Fine. Enjoy your rations." And I turned to leave.

"Ms. Orion, sometimes the strangest paths take us exactly where we need to be," Miles called out.

"Whatever," I muttered and waved at the guard. "I'm done here."

The guard gave me a sharp nod and returned to his post.

Once again, Miles wasn't being helpful, which honestly made me wonder if anything about him was. Maybe the setup with the smart-bots and the Star Eaters had been a coincidence, or Miles was someone's puppet and he wasn't helping because he didn't have anything to give me.

I really hoped not. I wasn't sure I could add anyone else to my dance card at the moment. With Star Eaters,

Commandant Yilmaz and the entire IGJ, Lucas, Miles, and Cain, my plate was full.

Off to medical, I guess. Dr. Kell would be waiting. My conversations with Miles never took long, and as horrific as seeing Cain laid out in medical was, spending time with him was a lot more comforting than talking with Miles. That said something, either about how deranged and unsettling Miles was or how painfully optimistic I was determined to be about Cain's condition.

The medical bay had quieted down after our little picnic with the *Justus*, and I appreciated the privacy Dr. Kell had provided for Cain. He'd been placed on a bed in the corner, where the doctor could activate privacy screens. That time, when I entered medical, Dr. Kell stepped away from Cain and activated the screens.

"Any change?" I asked, unable to keep the hope out of my voice.

Dr. Kell turned and shook her head. "No. I'm afraid not. But his vital signs are holding, and there's no new neurological damage."

I didn't answer. Each time I visited, I hoped for a different response—not that day, it seemed.

"If it's alright, I'd like to sit with him for a bit," I said.

"Actually, I need to talk with you first, if that's alright, Captain?"

That was different. Dr. Kell never addressed me by that title.

"Sure." I shrugged.

"If you please." She gestured toward her office.

We both took a seat, and Dr. Kell cleared her throat. "Are we still on course for Dar?" she asked.

"Yup."

"Then we'll need to start your genetic modeling. At least, I'm working on the assumption you'll be attempting to go to Dar. Forgive me if I overstep. Dr. Ashter has continued to consult, and he mentioned the possibility."

Interesting. "That's fine. Miles had mentioned something about it before"—I shrugged—"well... before."

The corners of her mouth moved up a hair. *I knew it. She's not a fan. Maybe we could form an antifan club of the would-be emperor. We could make matching jumpsuits and everything.*

"You'll need a series of gene-mods. Three in total over the next two weeks. The process will, unfortunately, have to be rushed as I would have preferred at least a month, but it can be done with minimal risk within the timeframe we have to work with. Not to mention masking the smart-bots. But I believe I might have a solution for that problem."

I tried my best to listen, but the doctor vanished down a black hole of medical terminology that sounded like a bunch of gobbledygook. If you're curious about gene-mod procedures, there's a wealth of information out there. Just don't go to some street vendor, for Pluto's sake. Find a professional.

"Do you consent?"

I blinked and nodded. "Sure. Yeah, I consent."

I didn't care too much about knowing all the horrible side effect possibilities—didn't need to add those to the list of things causing nightmares. Besides, I wasn't doing it for me. I was going to Dar for Cain, which meant doing whatever it took.

If a miracle occurred, and he woke up, and Dr. Kell could help him, then maybe we would table the whole vacation on Dar for a later date and focus on the bigger issue at hand. But right then, what I needed was to help Cain. I wasn't sure I wanted to face the "bigger issues" without him. I didn't want to be alone anymore.

"Ms. Orion?"

I jumped. "What? Oh, sorry."

Dr. Kell had stood at some point and come around her desk to lean against its edge. "Do you need to talk?"

The doctor had been patient with me, and I'd appreciated her noninvasive line of questions about the smart-bots. But I couldn't let myself open up to her. I didn't know if that was because of my memories of the string of therapists I'd seen after everything went down with my father or if I was hesitating to open up to someone else with the threat of losing Cain hanging over me.

Slippery eels. Look at me, now I'm psychoanalyzing myself. Good grief.

"No, I'm fine doc. The gene-mods?"

She frowned but didn't push. "We can start today if you're ready."

I pushed myself up out of the chair. "Let's do it."

The procedure didn't take long, and I sat with Cain for a time before heading out. I decided to head back to my rooms and lie low while the rest of the side effects cleared my system.

[DO YOU REQUIRE MEDICAL ASSISTANCE? YOUR

MOVEMENTS ARE ERRATIC, YOUR BLOOD PRESSURE IS ELE-VATED, AND YOUR HEART RATE IS HIGH FOR NO LOGGED CARDIO ACTIVITY.]*

No, I'm fine, I responded just as my stomach rolled and I leaned against the corridor's wall for support. *Really. Doc said the effects would wear off.*

I stumbled into my room in time to rush to the bathroom and throw up. I'll spare you the grisly details. But to sum it up, Dr. Kell had cautioned me that the gene-mods presented serious side effects for the first hour. Then the effects would vanish, and I would be right as rain.

Thirteen minutes to go. The doc had wanted me to stay in medical, but for a reason I can't remember now, I'd insisted on coming back to my hab-unit. I suspected Sam was providing the doc with continuous updates.

Believe it or not, the doc was right. One second, I was doubled over in cramps, and the next, poof, right as rain. *Not really looking forward to the next two rounds of that junk.* But I reminded myself it was for a good cause as I took a quick peek in the mirror—no differences yet. She'd told me I wouldn't see any noticeable changes until after the second treatment.

And I suddenly had a ton of time on my hands. *Great.*

"Sam, can you bring up ChowHo records?" I figured I might as well get started on Dr. Ashter's little assignment. *No time like the present.*

"Please specify."

"Start with a timeline of the company. Add the bios of its founders and present CEO and board members."

The Sur-T Screen lit up as the *Samaritan*'s AI network

opened document after document. I pulled up a chair and scrolled through them. Piles of information were there, so much that my head spun from it all. They'd formed ChowHo after three competing insurance groups had banded together as humanity moved beyond its colony on Mars. A high volume of turnover had been recorded among top-level management for several years until they went through a significant period of relative calm.

Igno Su Cho had been the CEO for well over forty years. *Impressive.* Then my eyes dropped to the next line. *Oh, wait. Never mind.* He'd been a cousin to the emperor of Old Earth, which wasn't surprising, given how many human corporations and businesses the monarchy funded and eventually took over. *Fingers in too many pies.*

After Igno, the rest of the CEOs had been all related, and the board of directors had become a publicity front. They didn't affect any genuine policy changes or oversight, but the media focused on the people if any scandal came up.

That was what led to the surprising bit. ChowHo Insurance hadn't had a major lawsuit in years, like almost fifty years. That was unheard of. Even with unending lines of credits, I had to believe there'd been someone out there unwilling to take a bribe, who would stand against the system in the name of the little guy.

I wasn't entirely sure I liked the implications.

"Sam, what can you find that might be off the record? Stories the media downplayed or didn't pick up?"

After a few minutes, Sam popped up new information on the screen.

"That's it?"

"Suggestion would be to broaden your parameters," the AI responded.

I was about ready to get up and move around—try to loosen some kind of lead—when a thought struck me like a meteoroid.

"Are there any records or media connecting Mrs. Fairhaven Gol with ChowHo Insurance or anyone prominent within ChowHo?"

The wait wasn't long before a new article popped up on the screen. *Bingo.*

A Fresh Face for the Board of Directors
By Lilly Sunder, NewsCorp Now

Out with the old and in with the new. A promising new start for ChowHo's board of directors wizened leadership at the dawn of a new age. Mrs. Fairhaven Gol, the esteemed CEO of Variant Solutions and former CEO of her family's generational company, Faithful, joins the board of ChowHo insurance next week.

Mrs. Gol presents out-of-the-box solutions with astounding results. What will she bring to the insurance world? Time will tell.

Stay tuned for more updates.

The article had copious advert snippets at the end. I was once again stuck with more questions than answers. *Except…*

"Sam, which insurance company oversaw the tours on the *Rapscallion*?"

"ChowHo Insurance."

That solved that mystery. It explained how the insane little old lady was able to set up a whole holo trip down memory lane.

What I didn't want to acknowledge, but had to, was that Mrs. Gol really had known my father. She'd shown me the whole matching tattoo and all, but I hadn't wanted to truly believe. All that nonsense felt as though it'd happened ages before, and despite everything, I'd held onto a sliver of hope about Pops.

Not anymore.

He could've been introduced to Mrs. Gol during his employment with ChowHo and sucked into the whole mixed-up sun-tattoo group, but the more likely answer was they'd known each before that and she'd secured his employment for him. I was assuming that because of what she told me on the *Rapscallion*.

I remembered her saying my father had been the best of them until he'd gone and polluted the gene pool with me and my brother.

I wasn't sure I could draw any other conclusion. The sun-tattoo group was into genetic purity or at least some kind of genetic purification. And if she considered my father the best of them, then the logical conclusion was that she'd been referencing his side of the family, because if my brother and I "polluted" the gene pool, then that had to be referring to my mother. *Great*. So Pops's entire side of the family had flown the coop and believed in all that junk.

I had to get up and stretch—then pace. *That doesn't make any sense, though. On a couple levels.* I'd met my father's folks. They weren't anything special, not in job or society or anything. Average workers on Old Earth, nose-to-the-grindstone types, they certainly weren't from Mrs. Gol's level of society.

And if Pops was a part of a selective group, why did he marry my mom?

"What did you do?" I asked, thoroughly frustrated.

"Please restate the question."

I sighed. "No, I wasn't talking to you. I'm just so angry at my father and this whole mess."

I suppose it's time, I thought. I'd put off searching for clues about my father's actions, not really ready to face what might come up. But I couldn't hide any longer.

"Sam, could you—"

The door chime went off.

"Who is it?" I asked Sam.

"It's Commander Lio."

4

Bad News or Worse News? Your Choice.

Typically, Commander Lio was physically imposing, with an aura of quiet strength. His unofficially taking over the duties of the captain had brought a calm to the crew after having witnessed their captain killed by the IGJ. But Lio was visibly agitated as he stepped into my hab-unit. An unsettled energy radiated off him, and if that wasn't giveaway enough, then the tufts of hair, from his Telt side of the family, standing up on end should've been.

"Commander?" I asked.

Lio looked everywhere but at me. *Uh-oh. That bad, huh?*

He moved and stood in front of the window, gazing out into the blackness of space. "We've received word. Starbase 9.2 and the outer rims of Cloud-11 have been…" He stopped then turned to face me. "Destroyed."

My mouth opened, but no words came out. I stumbled back and dropped into a chair. "That's not… I mean…"

"Possible?" Lio said and gestured toward a chair.

When I gave him a weak nod, he sat. "Lucas showed it was."

I took a deep breath and focused on what Lio was telling me.

"Reports are stating the areas of destruction are showing a complete loss. There wasn't any warning for anyone to evacuate."

"Why?" I asked through clenched teeth. "Is he claiming responsibility for it?" Even using the pronoun in place of his name felt as if I was tasting poison.

"Yes. He's reporting the Jumjul were taking action, and this is the consequence. But the Jumjul have issued a statement that it's all lies. They weren't preparing any type of attack."

He held my gaze for a moment then dropped his. "We're already seeing mobs form, calling on military forces and the IGJ to do something. But there's a thousand different whispers as to what government is gearing up, who might pull away… It's the beginning of chaos."

"The bastard said he wanted a war," I whispered and abruptly stood.

"If that's what he wanted, then he's succeeding. But besides him, the biggest threat is the Jumjul. No one knows how they'll react or who they'll retaliate against. Humanity, most likely."

"Thank you for telling me," I said as I paced back and forth. When he didn't move, I stopped and turned toward him. "But that's not all, is it?"

Lio stood and shook his head. "No. Even the best of crews in the worst of times can have… difficulties. A handful of my officers are from Cloud-11 or have family ties there. I would advise it would be best to stay—"

"In my room? Is that it? Because I share a last name with the crazy lunatic, they'll transfer their rage to me? Been there, done that." I straightened. "And I won't do it again."

I stepped close to Lio and looked him straight in the eye. "I hid and cowered after my father was arrested, and look where that got me. Nowhere. Isolated and cut off from the things I should've been paying attention to. I'm not doing that again. I'm not burying my head in the sand anymore."

A hint of concern showed on the commander's face, before he schooled his features into neutrality. "I sympathize. But I am still recommending you stay in your room. Or at least, keep out of the heavily trafficked areas until I've talked with the crew."

I scowled. The commander had a valid point. Emotions and tensions would be running high. *Why should I add fuel to the fire? Except why shouldn't I be able to move about as I want, do what I want? I've got nothing to do with my brother's actions.*

Or do you? A pesky little voice asked. No, it wasn't Cain or Sam but my own stupid little mind playing with me.

"Fine. I'll consider your suggestion. Is that all?" I asked.

Lio nodded. "Yes. I'll keep you updated as events unfold."

"Good."

Before Lio left, I stopped him. "Look. Thank you

for personally coming and telling me. And I'll take your recommendation seriously."

Lio's features softened. "I'm not without sympathy. But my first duty is to the ship and its crew."

I nodded. "I know. Thank you, Lio."

Lio left, and I stood there, alone with my thoughts and desperately wishing I wasn't. <*Cain, if you're out there, somewhere, please… I need you.*>

Cain had been with me when I discovered the truth about my father, and he hadn't turned away. I wanted to believe that he wouldn't now, either—that at least I would have someone who believed in me.

Against my better judgement, I watched the reports until my eyes were puffy from too many tears. My brother, the boy I'd grown up with, who'd been my sole companion for years, had turned into a hideous harbinger of death. His name and face were plastered everywhere, along with my father's. Not to mention the rampant gossip and theories as to what their ultimate motivation was. Each newscast I watched spiraled further into insanity.

Hoping they would keep my name out of the reports was wishful thinking. People had dug up my employment history. Images of my apartment were posted everywhere, and even a few pictures from inside my apartment popped up. It was a pretty sure bet that I wouldn't ever be going back.

A few reporters tried to interview Weplies who worked with Confore Tech, but their questions were ignored, and they promptly threw out the brave few who tried to get past security at the building.

I couldn't help but wonder if Confore didn't want to talk about its employees per their strict policies on employee privacy—one reason I worked for Confore—or if they were afraid of prying questions that might uncover the truth about the SeeClear tech.

But that wasn't the worst of it. The worst was Commandant Yilmaz.

She held a press conference and stated the IGJ's sympathies were with the families who'd suffered such tragic losses. Then she looked straight down the barrel of the camera and said she was determined to bring the perpetrators to justice: Lucas Orion and his associates, including his sister.

"You frigid old hag!" I shouted at the Sur-T Screen. After screaming a bit more and throwing a few things, I stormed out of my room. I didn't give a damn about anyone else's feelings, and if they had an issue with me, they'd better be ready to fight.

My nuclear-reactor-sized storm kept everyone at bay as I prowled the ship. I marched down to medical, stood in front of the doors, then decided I couldn't enter. Seeing Cain would have probably broken me. Instead, I wound my way through the ship.

My stomach rumbled. I ignored it. Then it rumbled again, and I grumbled but decided some food might calm me down. Maybe I wouldn't achieve calm, but I could drown my fury in a whole smorgasbord of goodies.

The commissary on Deck Twelve had too many people. The doors opened, and I stood there. A few looked up and sneered. One young woman stood before her companions pulled her back down. I was tempted to storm in there, order from the food dispensers, and take a seat, to force them to be around me.

But for all my bravado, I couldn't—too many eyes, as well as hushed voices talking about me. I wanted to be brave, to show them their opinions didn't matter, that I knew who I was.

I spun around and left.

I didn't know. Fears and worries and doubts all jostled for first place. *Will I become like my brother or my father once I learn the truth? Am I only good because I've kept myself isolated? What if digging all this stuff up makes me turn out like them?*

My feet slowed as my stomach churned. I wasn't hungry anymore. When I finally came to a stop, I was on Deck Fifteen. *Stupid subconscious.*

Do I want to know what in the rec hall Miles thought was worth seeing? Do I have a choice?

My father's voice rang through my thoughts without prompting. *"Don't be foolish. Of course you have a choice. I would be proud to sponsor you at the Eeag schooling branch. If that's what you want to do, I'll make the arrangements. But if you want to stay with me and your brother, I'd be proud of that choice too."*

I'd been eleven, the age of admission into prereq courses to use for applications to secondary schooling branches. I hadn't ever given it much thought until we'd worked on Selarious the year before the Cricade Wars began. Two other families were there at the site—a rarity—and I'd become enamored with the other girls.

They'd been on vacation, a break between finishing their primary schooling branch and prepping for secondary. And because they'd gone to a primary schooling branch, they could bypass the prereq courses.

Both of the girls had been refined, at least to my eleven-year-old eyes. The contrast between my self-image and how they carried themselves, able to discuss topics I couldn't, had made me feel like nothing but a mud worm. They didn't join their parents at the dig site—neither wanted to get dirty—and spent their time studying or gossiping. So I'd searched and read all about secondary schooling branches and settled on Eeag. The schooling branch furthest away from xenology. I would choose a career in agriculture.

My father surely knew what was behind my rants and tears, and he no doubt also knew I ultimately wouldn't leave. I loved my life. I really did. I gave him props for the fact that he hadn't forced me either way. I believe he would've truly supported me if I'd left.

Nobody knew what my life would've been like if I'd followed through with the Eeag.

Maybe I could admit Wats wasn't all bad—not with how he'd raised me, anyway. I knew he'd loved me. And I knew he'd loved Lucas even though they'd never had a strong relationship. Perhaps I'd inherited the good and Lucas the bad. I know that's a pretty simplistic way to look at it, but that was all the positivity I could muster.

I decided if I was going to prove to myself and the rest of the known worlds that I wasn't my father or my brother, I needed to keep working on figuring out what was going on.

So I played along with Miles's little game and stepped into the rec hall on Deck Fifteen.

5

Star Eaters

I screamed.

You would have, too, considering how high tensions were running.

My first impression, as the lights flickered on, was that I'd stepped into a meeting of Star Eaters. But after my rather impressive bellow, none of the robes moved. Not figures—robes.

The rec hall was lined with Star Eater robes hanging off mannequins.

"What is that scummy scuttle crab caught in a jelly's pod playing at?"

[Your heart rate is elevated. Do you require assistance?]

No. I'm fine.

I needed a good several minutes before my heart rate settled enough for me to take another step forward. Cautiously, I moved through the room, counting twelve robes in total.

As the shock wore off, I noted various displays behind each robe, and I reached out and touched one of the screens. It lit up and scrolled through a plethora of information. I had to go through it twice to catch all the major points. After reading a handful of other display screens, I realized what I was looking at.

At first, my mind had leaped to one horrible possibility: Miles was a member of the Star Eater cult—or even their leader. That thought tracked with the trickery on Lunar 5. Or instead, the whole cult deal could've been a cover for more nefarious business Miles conducted. That would certainly fit the profile for the crazy man.

But the information I read painted quite a different picture. And to be honest, that bummed me out. If Miles had been behind the Star Eaters, that would've wrapped everything up into a neat little mess.

On the displays were dates and locations. A few I recognized, but most of them I didn't. For each of those, detailed information was included on how each robe was acquired. But none of the information talked about *who* or *what* had been wearing the robes. No bodies, corpses, or injured were ever in the area, just a discarded robe, despite the best attempt of each mission to secure a Star Eater.

Numerous tests and biological samples had been taken from the robes, but all results had come back inconclusive.

Okay, clever would-be emperor, you have my attention.

I read through the displays one more time then trudged back to Central Processing.

"Spill it," I snapped.

Miles was stretched out on the cot, hands behind his head, his eyes closed.

"I know you're not asleep," I said. "I visited your little hall of fame."

One eye popped open, then another, and a huge grin split his face. "Like it? Took quite a few years to snag that grand of a collection." He sat up then sprang up off the cot. "Do you know the black-market price of each robe? Of even a piece of a robe? You could buy a small moon for that amount of credits."

"There's something inherently wrong with you, isn't there?"

Miles shrugged. "Maybe. Don't know. My aunties were never quite right in the head. Come to think of it, my father had a weakness for—"

"Stop," I said. "I don't want to hear your sordid family history."

"Another time." He sniffed.

"The robes?"

"Right, of course, my dear. The robes. I'm assuming you caught the juicy little tidbit about no bodies being recovered?"

I nodded.

"But that's not entirely true."

I took a step forward. "Explain."

"The fascination with the Star Eater cult began right after their first appearance, and the moniker was coined. And ever since then, there are individuals and groups who have dedicated their lives to figuring out just what exactly the Star Eater cult is all about."

"I suspected that after talking with Dr. Ashter."

Miles shook his head. "Our clever little doctor isn't researching the Star Eater cult."

I frowned. "What? Are you feeling alright?"

"Never better." To prove his point, he hopped around a bit like a fool then stopped as close to the barrier as he could get, and a wide grin split his face in two.

"Dr. Ashter is researching the Star Eaters. Not the Star Eater cult. Seems he has you barking up the wrong tree."

I'll admit I took longer than I would have liked to catch on to what Miles was telling me. But when I did, it clicked.

"Pluto's slippery eels."

"You got it, my buttery little biscuit."

Of course a difference would exist. Fanatical fan groupies were a staple throughout human history and were not unique to humanity. Several other species had the tendency to do the same thing, to idolize a group or individual to the point of creepyville.

"So the question is, who were the Star Eaters I've interacted with? Or that my father had contact with? Crazy groupies or the real deal?"

"An excellent question. Although I suspect we both know the answer."

"Miles, I swear you'd better give me answers, or I'll—"

"You'll what? Toss me out of an airlock? I think not. You might keep me here for a while longer, but admit it, you need me."

I huffed. The bugger was right. Miles held too many pieces of that annoying puzzle. Or at least, he still had the potential to. He was great at bluffing, but I doubted he was that time, not with his wealth and connections.

He had Dr. Ashter working for him, along with the unnerving collection of robes. Miles knew a lot more than what he was telling me.

I calmed down enough to not scream at the man. "Fine. You've got me there. But what's up with the veiled hints about Dr. Ashter? He's been nothing but helpful. You could learn a thing or two from him, you know."

Miles shrugged. "He's a man of many secrets. You don't live as long as he has without them. But I would wager he's a touch jealous. He doesn't have the claim to fame you do. Or your father."

Pop my little bubble of hope that someone was on my side, why don't you? But that didn't mean Dr. Ashter wasn't, just that he was being as cagey as the rest. Or he was warming up to something or waiting to see what information I would give him before he gave me anything of value. *Surprise, surprise.*

"Until you provide me with solid information, not treasure hunts or cryptic word puzzles, you're stuck where you are."

Miles grinned and sat down on his cot. "I can wait."

I stepped closer, with a thought. "Can you? Has anyone updated you?"

I took a bit of pride in watching his smile slip just a tad.

"I'll take that as a no. My brother has seen fit to do a tad bit more redecorating throughout the known worlds. The outer reaches of Cloud-11 and Starbase 9.2."

I'd guessed right. The news hit a nerve, just as it had with Lunar 5. *So there is a heart in there somewhere.*

"Survivors?"

The pride I'd felt vanished as the anguish in his eyes was real. I shook my head. *What am I playing at?* "No," I said softly. "Complete losses."

Miles stood and moved as far away from me as he could get in the tiny cell. "My sister's family settled down on Cloud-11 after they—" He stopped. "It doesn't matter, I guess."

I didn't want to, but I felt sympathy for him. "I'm sorry. Do you know where, exactly? Maybe they're still okay."

"The inner rings. Only the best, right?"

"Hold on." *Sam. Any new information on Cloud-11?*

[The outer reaches of Cloud-11 currently reporting complete destruction or significant damage are Leanora's Leap, Jump Ten, Whister's Balcony, and Blue Skies. None of the inner rings are reporting any significant damage, although it is believed debris fields will pose a significant problem in the next few days. Basil's Ledge and Rainbow Ruins are currently under evacuation orders. Further evacuation orders are believed to be forthcoming.]

I reached out to steady myself but found sliding to the floor was a much better option as my head spun with the information. I'd never been to Cloud-11—too wealthy for my taste. But the rings were absolutely breathtaking, taking the best of Old Earth's once-vibrant ecosystems and replicating them with a mix of exotic alien plant and animal life, not to mention the unusual architecture and hypnotizing vistas.

"Basil's Ledge and Rainbow Ruins are on evac orders.

It sounds like someone will issue more orders soon," I said.

Following my lead, Miles sat on the floor of his cell and let his head flop back against the wall. "The last I knew, they'd taken up residence on River's Dusting. But they could have moved since then. That was… years ago." After a significant pause, he said a small "thank you."

I didn't respond but sat there in silence with him until the guard got nervous and poked his head around the corner to check on us. I smiled and waved him off.

"What now?" I asked, not really expecting an answer.

"The Star Eaters are a species we don't understand—the true Star Eaters. My theories lie in looking at the different religions across the known worlds. You'll find some interesting similarities peppered throughout, not to mention the mythology.

"While I've had dealings with what I believe to be the actual alien species, it's only ever been through messages and comms. I've never been graced by their physical appearance. But I know they only travel in pairs. That's a big clue to how to differentiate between the Star Eaters and the cult members."

My turn to be blown out of an airlock. I hadn't expected a straight answer from him.

I twisted around on the floor to look at him. "Thank you, Miles."

He nodded.

"Pairs, huh? Then you're implying I've actually had contact with them."

He nodded again.

"What makes me so special?"

He shrugged. "I don't know. Maybe because of the connection with your father? And yes, I know about that."

I narrowed my eyes as a realization hit me. I should have been angry, furious even, with him, but emotionally, I was worn out. "So you injected me with these smart-bots, sent me off to meet actual Star Eaters, and didn't have a clue as to what was going to happen?"

He closed his eyes. "Yes. The price was worth the risk."

I could have stormed off. I should have stormed off. But I sat there and stared at him. If my life was worth risking when something was obviously special about me, or at least my father's connection with that enigmatic species, then I had no idea what kind of horrible, twisted stakes he was playing for.

6

No Matter What

During the next several days, I picked up a few more bits and pieces of information from Miles and Dr. Ashter. I saw no point in keeping Miles in the brig any longer—that had been a foolish impulse on my part to teach him a lesson. He isolated himself for a few days, and I assumed he was catching up with the news and political upheavals.

We were all glued to the news.

The Jumjul were dusting off their military gear, and warship patrols throughout several sectors had increased. Minor skirmishes were reported on half a dozen worlds and outposts, and most governments were desperately trying to maintain control. Riots and crime had increased exponentially as individuals and groups took advantage of the chaos and grief.

I listened to Cain's mother, Chancellor Heron, speak a few times. She listed the different places that were open for evacuees and condemned the actions of Lucas and the Sun Worshipers. That's what the media were dubbing them—not particularly inventive, but it worked.

I caught reports of security protocols being changed or added, to scan individuals to see if they carried the tattoo. And I noticed an alarming uptick in individuals proudly claiming to be a part of the purist movement, finding back-alley parlors still willing to tattoo that particular image. I was thanking my lucky stars my father had never allowed me to get that tattoo.

The only good event that happened as we traveled to Dar was when we were less than two days out of hitting the edge of Dar-controlled space.

*[M*R*. T*UREN ED*-S*UREN HAS WOKEN UP*. D*R*. K*ELL WOULD LIKE YOU TO COME TO MEDICAL AS SOON AS POSSIBLE.]*

I'd been knee-deep in Dar history and local customs, courtesy of Dr. Ashter, when Sam alerted me. I don't think I'd ever moved that fast in my life. I rushed into the medical bay only to come to a screeching halt to stare at Cain, awake and answering Dr. Kell's questions.

<*You're okay.*> I thought with an overwhelming sense of relief. I expected an answer but got none. *That's alright—he's busy focusing on Dr. Kell,* I reassured myself.

She glanced up, saw me, and motioned me over. I wasn't sure I believed what I saw. *Perhaps I'm dreaming.* But when Cain turned his head to stare at me, his liquid violet eyes looking me over, I shivered. It was real. He was going to be okay.

Without thinking, I closed the gap between us and flung my arms around him. Tears poured down my face. "I knew you would be okay. I didn't give up. I couldn't." I mumbled into his shoulder. When his hands didn't reach up to return the hug, I pulled back, slightly embarrassed.

Then I realized how odd I must've looked. We'd finished the course of gene-mods, and I was visibly a Darquet. A soft cranial ridge had formed above my eyes, which tapered back toward my ears. Purple-hued skin with patches of scales trailed along my cheeks and down my neck.

"Geez. I'm sorry. This must be a shock to you. We've been doing a series of gene-mods so I can—"

Cain cut me off, turning his focus back to Dr. Kell. "You were saying?"

She glanced at me but quickly turned toward Cain. "Now that you're awake, we can begin experimenting with a course of drugs to help with the neurological damage, specifically regarding the telepathic connection you share with Ms. Orion. There's no guarantee it will fully restore the connection, but I'm confident we'll be able to repair most of those areas responsible for such an ability. We'll also address the physical damage as well—"

"No. I'll heal as I am. What's done is done."

I gaped at him. "Surely, you don't mean that."

"Doctor, I appreciate all you've done. But I would like to rest now."

Dr. Kell nodded and threw me a sympathetic look as she turned to leave.

"You're not serious, are you?" I asked.

"I would ask you to leave as well. I need to rest."

<Cain? What's going on?>

But he gave no response, not even a twitch of an eyebrow to indicate he'd heard me. My chest tightened, and a nervous flutter of anxiety settled in my gut.

"Look, we're only a few days out from Dar. I'm going

to get a heart stone. Then everything will be okay. We'll figure out a way through this. Together, right?"

Cain rolled his head to one side and stared at me. I could see a struggle on his face, but he decided not to say whatever he was thinking. Instead, he turned away and remained silent.

Isn't he happy to see me?

"Mahia? Would you come to my office for a moment?"

I walked over to Dr. Kell's desk in a daze. "What's wrong with him?"

"Please sit," she said.

She smiled softly, but I noticed it didn't reach her eyes. They held only pity. I didn't want her pity. I wanted to know what was wrong with Cain.

"He's been through a very traumatic time—not just the neurological damage, but the physical as well. Everyone responds differently, but I think in his case, it would be best if you gave him time. Visit him, support him, but know his recovery will be difficult, not just physically but emotionally as well. Now that he's awake, Dr. Felto will visit with him."

I frowned.

"He's a psychiatrist and a former licensed counselor for the military. I believe his experience will be beneficial for Mr. Suren ed-Turen."

Nothing was wrong with what Dr. Kell was saying, and I knew that. But I'd pinned many of my hopes on Cain waking up and giving me the emotional support I craved. I hadn't stopped to consider what he would need instead.

I wanted to stay, to just sit with him. But I honored

his request and wandered the ship for hours after I left medical. Eventually, though, I made my way back to medical. We had only a few days before I left for Dar, and I would clearly be going on my own. Everyone who'd been a part of the planning had hoped Cain would wake soon enough to regain his strength and travel with me. Last week, we'd had to make other plans. Even if Cain had woken up then, a week wouldn't have been long enough to help him build up his strength and go through a gene-mod treatment to obscure his human side.

Dr. Ashter had declined, stating he'd reached the physical limit of gene-mods his body could handle. *And Miles...* Despite his shift from flippant to serious, I didn't want him with me. Surprisingly enough, he didn't put up a fight. We threw around the names of several *Samaritan* officers to go with me, but I eventually decided going alone would be best.

So the plan was that I would travel to Dar under the assumed identity of Serea el-Merea, the granddaughter of Kaom ed-Paom, an ambassador of Dar who'd been assigned to the far-flung world of Eshi Racc, where transmissions went to die.

The cover story Miles and Dr. Ashter had dreamed up, worked on, and labored over was adequate. If an inquiring mind within Dar security or the military dug deep, they would undoubtedly find the holes. But for my purposes, it would have to do.

Because of the isolation of Eshi Racc, it was plausible Kaom and his family had either not been aware of the growing isolation of their people, or considering the vastness of space, the journey to return to their home world simply took time and more than a few detours. And along with those detours, his grandchildren had picked up some unbecoming fascinations with human culture. The simple explanation would help me maneuver through any cultural faux pas.

Kaom ed-Paom was a real person. He'd been an ambassador, though minor and with no notable accolades. The reports stated he'd been newly married at the time of his posting to Eshi Racc, and because of infrequent reports, only speculation could be made regarding the number of children Kaom had, and nothing about any potential grandchildren.

That created the perfect in for me.

I didn't want to be impervious to Cain's request to rest, but I didn't know what the future might hold. And I needed to be with him even if that meant sitting in a corner, staring at him. I would hold on to the knowledge he was alive and burn the image of him into my mind. When everything went sideways—truthfully, we all knew the mission wasn't going to go according to plan—I would use my memories to push me through whatever was going to happen. Because I knew one thing: I was going to succeed. Whether our relationship was forever altered or not, I was going to find a heart stone and make sure Cain had every chance to recover.

And a part of that recovery would be finding and rescuing his sister. I hadn't discussed that little detour in the plans with Dr. Ashter or Miles. However, I thought the sneaky little scuttle crab suspected a bit more going on behind my beautiful eyes than I'd let on.

Too bad, scuttle crab. Too bad.

7

Decisions, Decisions

[DAR MILITARY HAS ISSUED A WARNING. IF WE DON'T CHANGE COURSE WITHIN THE NEXT THIRTY-ONE HOURS, THEY WILL FIRE UPON US.]

We'd hit our first snag.

Commander Lio attempted to negotiate with the military, stating they had a Darquet aboard who'd come a long way in order to get home. But the military didn't care. I suppose if my brother and his cronies hadn't gone on a killing spree, we might have had a hair's width of a chance that the military would negotiate. But everyone was spooked.

When negotiations didn't work, Lio sent orders for Dr. Ashter, Miles, me, and the commanding officers to gather in the captain's lounge. I stayed in the back, leaning against a wall and listening to everyone's input.

Most of the officers argued for turning around to help fight against the Sun Worshipers. While they were aware that we were on our way to Dar in order to help Cain, bringing the Sun Worshipers to justice was a higher priority. I couldn't find any fault with their arguments. If I'd had family threatened or killed by Lucas and his lot, I would be out for blood as well.

For a split second, I wondered if I was doing the right thing, putting my needs ahead of so many others'. The *Samaritan* was an impressive ship. No doubt, it would've been a benefit in the fight against Lucas. But I couldn't abandon Cain.

Is it smart to focus on Cain right now? I could work on unraveling several tangents if we did turn around. We could rendezvous with the Master Glipglow and work on deciphering my smart-bots and what they were doing to me. Or I could delve into the world of Lucas and figure out his goal and help bring him to justice—not to mention the endless hours of research that could be done, regarding the Star Eaters.

"If we turn back, we can work with any number of alliances. There are more than a handful who would gladly take us in. And with the current situation, the IGJ has better things to do than hunt us," one of the officers said.

"I agree," another added. "The IGJ aren't a concern right now. Even if they did try to arrest us—and for what, honestly?—public sentiment would be on our side."

"You seem to forget that the *Samaritan* hasn't been flashed to the media. We've been operating in the dark ever since the unfortunate ending of the *Rapscallion*," Miles interjected. "If we reveal ourselves now, the worlds would only wonder what other things Old Earth might be hiding."

"But we're not aligned with Old Earth," the officer shot back.

I hadn't really given too much thought as to where their allegiances lay. I'd been working under the assumption Miles employed them. But I didn't know where they'd come from originally. I wondered if a crew like that would be able to stay together in that situation.

The one thing I was sure of was that they'd come from military backgrounds. Those officers had been trained to fight. And they were being asked whether they should stay on the sidelines and potentially add a little more chaos to the worlds if we ticked off Dar.

Miles stood and gave a flowery speech that would've rivaled any emperor's. But I gave him a few points for sticking to his end of the agreement, at least, saying we were heading for Dar and that was final. But his wrap-up gave me chills.

"Each one of you has signed a contract, and I will hold you to the terms of said contract. If you choose to break our agreement, understand this." Miles swept his eyes across the room, his expression deadly. "I will find you."

A ripple of unhappy—even mutinous—looks passed throughout the room before Lio stood. I felt for him. He'd been trying to run the ship as a captain who valued the input of his crew, but Miles reminded them that wasn't reality. He was ultimately in charge.

I shifted my weight and pushed off the wall. I swear I didn't make a sound, but all eyes turned toward me. I'm not sure what came over me, but I had a thousand different heartfelt pleas rolling around in my head. I wanted them to understand that going to Dar wasn't because of Miles, that they were doing it because I was asking them to turn away from their loved ones and home worlds on the off chance that I might help Cain.

But instead of speaking, I turned and left.

I'd made my decision.

I headed to medical and was glad it was relatively empty when I arrived. I took a chair and sat next to Cain's bed and stayed there in the silence for some time. I watched his chest slowly rise and fall, my eyes tracing the outline of his body, curled up on his side, turned toward me.

Tears slipped down my cheeks, and I bit my lip to keep from crying out. I leaned forward and gently laid a hand over his.

"You were there for me when you could have walked away. You saw the worst, heard the horrors my father committed, yet stayed by my side. You could have let me die or turned me over to the IGJ for further questioning or even scientific study. You really should have. I'm sure that would've helped boost your ranking, and then you never would've gotten into this mess. But you didn't. Not even on the *Justus* when they—" I had to stop for a minute as the words clogged my throat. *Pesky emotions.*

I squeezed his hand, stood, and leaned over him, letting my forehead rest against his. He wasn't asleep anymore, and I didn't care. I didn't know if he could hear me, but I couldn't bring myself to speak the rest of what I needed to say out loud.

<*I don't know what you went through on the* Justus *except*

for what Yilmaz forced me to watch. I can't imagine what any of it must have been like. And I'm assuming they gave you the chance to give me up, or even Miles, to say or do something that would've restored your ranking within the IGJ. Any words I can say would be weak compared to the magnitude of your injuries, but thank you. Thank you for staying with me through the horror of it all. So while my words can't make up for much, my actions can. I swear to you I will make sure you get everything you need in order to heal.>

I paused then pulled back just enough to kiss him. I desperately wanted to say a few other words, but I couldn't as the tears refused to stop. As I straightened and turned to go, Cain squeezed my hand.

I feared what I might see if I turned to look at him. I almost didn't. *But if a chance existed—of something—I had to know.* Slowly, I turned. Cain's eyes were open, and a beautiful amber light shone back at me.

I stood there, mesmerized by the warmth and pain wrapped in his beautiful amber eyes. And I drank in every single drop of those emotions, tucked them inside my own, then squeezed his hand one more time, turned, and left.

Sam, I'm going to need a shuttle. Something away from prying eyes.

After the briefest of pauses, Sam came through for me.

[A SHUTTLE WILL BE PREPPED. AWAITING FURTHER ORDERS.]

When I got to my rooms, Miles was waiting for me.

"There's no use in trying to talk you out of it, is there?" he asked.

I wiped my tears away and shook my head. "There is not."

"Then my only advice is to tread carefully. Dar is… complicated on several levels. I'm not sure yet if the cosmos is playing some kind of horrid joke on you by bringing you here."

If my mind hadn't been scattered in a thousand different directions, I might've caught the hidden implication of classic Miles knowing more than he was saying.

"Do the others suspect?" I asked.

"No. Well, Dr. Ashter might. He's dealt with Orions before, but command? No, they don't. Lio and the others are too focused on what's happening out there to pay much attention to what's going on in here."

"I think that's a rather shortsighted view of Commander Lio," I said.

Miles shrugged. "Perhaps."

I stopped moving about the room and turned to face Miles. "Watch over him. Please."

He nodded and moved to stand in front of me. He reached out and traced a finger down the side of my head. "I promise." Then, with a forlorn shake of his head, Miles left.

I didn't have much prep. Everything had already been taken care of. We'd customized a few outfits and trinkets to help shore up my assumed identity. So I changed from my cozy jumpsuit into a slightly outdated set of clothes emulating Dar fashion, hoping it would send just the right message.

Jupiter's moons. Where are these tears coming from? This isn't some jute-store story. Get it together.

I sniffed, wiped away another onslaught of tears, and marched over to the bags. After one last look around the hab-unit, I slung the straps of the bags over my shoulder and headed out.

Thankfully, the corridors were fairly empty. Sam, the crafty little AI, had picked a hangar on one of the lower decks with the least activity. The few crewmen I did pass paid me no attention. But the trick to that was walking with confidence. Head up, I moved forward with purpose. People didn't question me because I looked like I knew what I was doing.

That was a useful little tip I'd picked up from my father. He worked hard to go through all the proper channels, getting clearance to work at different sites, hiring help, and a host of other tasks. But that didn't mean he didn't bend the rules a little or bluff a bit here and there in order to get into the proper offices or meet with the right people.

The hangar was half lit when I arrived, and I hurried over to the shuttle Sam had indicated. I did a double take. Three shuttles were in the hangar, and mine had its exterior lights on.

"Sam? Is this thing even flightworthy?"

The outer hull was worn and sported more than a few dents. The shuttle's designation, *Jhan B-133*, meant it was one of the oldest classes of shuttles left in working order. I wasn't a ship guru or hobbyist, but I recognized the name, and I'm sure you did as well. But I'll recap just in case.

Adria Jhan was a brilliant engineer. Her name was well-known on a wide variety of worlds, not just human.

In the early years of human expansion, exploration, and building tentative alliances with the different species encountered, spacecraft were still being perfected.

On one particular mission, Jhan and the crew she was traveling with were conducting field tests of a prototype shield. They'd conducted all the requisite tests both in simulation and shorter test flights. With every confidence in the system, Jhan and the crew took to the stars.

The shielding held, and on their return trip, they encountered a severely damaged Glipglow ship. That wasn't a first-contact situation, but no formal alliance had been formed between humanity and Glipglows. Reports on exactly how communication went at first are limited.

I suspect a political cover-up because everything about the story is a little too tidy. And in other accounts of the first interactions between humans and Glipglows, readers will note a trend of misunderstanding leading to more than a dozen skirmishes. If you really want to get lost down a wormhole, look up the whisper nets where people dedicate their lives to trying to prove historical conspiracy theories.

With some miraculous and decidedly unorthodox maneuvers, Jhan changed the shielding to encompass the Glipglow vessel and stayed with the injured ship until they reached Glipglow space.

Glipglow masters who specialized in engineering and ship technology were so impressed that Jhan was allowed to become an honorary apprentice in Glipglow society. She would never actually be able to attain master status, though. Some cultural and species lines would never be crossed by the Glipglows. But the title and the gesture were extraordinary. That event also helped seal a formal relationship between the two species.

Supposedly, Jhan actually took up an apprenticeship with a Glipglow master a few years later. But no one has confirmed that.

Thus, despite the massive feat of engineering that went into all spacecraft, any shuttle designated with *Jhan* was old. And with the letter *B* as the version identifier, it was ancient. I wouldn't have questioned the AI's choice if the letter had been an *X* or even a *U*. I knew those models were at least still listed in ChowHo Insurance policies.

"All shuttles on the *Samaritan* are fully functional and fit for service," the AI replied.

"Uh-huh. Where in the world did you get this one?" I asked, not feeling any relief at the AI's brief and non-committal response.

"They brought it on board at the request of Zhu Akio."

I grinned. *Alright, then. Old and untrustworthy vessel it is.*

8

It's All or Nothing

Space is cold, dark, and vast. And it's extremely unnerving even though I'd only been in the shuttle for a little over ten hours. I hadn't expected the unease that settled over me. Space without reference points such as a planet or a moon can be overwhelming. The mind plays tricks in order to find balance and patterns in the pitch black. Even though I had sturdy walls surrounding me, my mind still knew exactly where I was and how precarious the situation could be, not to mention the doubt and anxiety that were gleefully taking turns.

So perhaps my plan wasn't the greatest idea I'd ever cooked up.

Maybe it was the worst or at least in the top ten of bad ideas—or top five.

Alright. It really was the worst.

The *Samaritan* contacted me several times, and I'd earned an extremely irate message from Commander Lio about putting his crew at risk, not following protocol, and refusing to see the bigger picture. All those issues aside, I think he got his fur ruffled because I hadn't turned over full command of the *Samaritan*.

That wasn't an oversight on my part. Sam was my backup plan. I wasn't ready to relinquish my biggest asset during the stupidest rock-tail-lobster-scummed plan, especially not after Sam confirmed our communications range was phenomenal. As long as the ship stayed within a range of two days—Old Earth standard—we would have communication with little to no delay.

I felt confident Miles wasn't about to lose track of his prize shuttle, either. Of course, I was hoping I ranked higher than the shuttle, considering all the time and effort he'd put into me. But Miles was Miles, and he was a wild card.

Speaking of which, I had a message from a very irritated Miles. He whined about how he considered my use of his shuttle a theft of a precious piece of history. I played that message innumerable times and grinned through the entire thing each time.

As I familiarized myself with the shuttle and read through the schematics—the tech was fairly straight forward, the nitty-gritty details boring—I realized how crafty the AI had been. Because of the age of the shuttle, it had no retrieval codes, no way for the AI to tie the shuttle's system to its own. And because of the shuttle's engine design, the tech was so out of date that the ship had no way to track me, either.

I was just another small potential blip on the *Samaritan*'s radar. Lio would have to guess which piece of potential blip I could be. So far, since no one had shown up on my radar, I'd gone with the assumption they'd been guessing wrong. Of course, the possibility was real that the crew could have mutinied, cut their losses, and turned Sam around to join the fight against my brother. But I hoped Sam, or at least Miles, would give me a heads-up if it came to that.

An even further sobering thought was that Sam could be messing with the crew and doctoring the ship's readouts. *Artificial Intelligence Monthly* wasn't the most popular magazine on the racks, but I would occasionally pick one up. It was worth the credits.

Loads of research had been done, studying the very real implication of AI tech developing sentience. For a large period of human history, it encouraged AI sentience development. The argument had been that artificial intelligence could sort through billions of calculations in a blink of an eye. A ship's AI could take over when and if a crew became incapacitated. But an emotional intelligence layered underneath all the algorithms might make the difference in a ship deciding what to do in order to protect its crew.

But the Jumjul and Glipglow governments were strictly against sentient AI. Both species had quite a few horror stories to back up their staunch stance against the tech, so humans had quieted down in that corner.

But at that moment, when I was heading for a potentially hostile situation with an AI ship backing me up, I didn't care. I would take all the help I could get. If Sam had an ounce of sentience and was deciding on her own, and that included protecting me, then all the better.

I didn't waste too many hours getting sucked down

that particular wormhole, though. I spent most of my time focusing on the files I'd downloaded and brought. I reviewed everything—language, customs, my artificial family lineage, the whole meringue-topped pie. By the time my shuttle tripped Dar security alarms, I was feeling more Darquet than human—a lost little lamb returning to the fold.

A light on the comms panel lit up, and with a deep breath, I pressed the button.

"Shuttle craft, identify," someone commanded.

"Honor and respect are given upon your lineage. This is the *Jhan B-133* requesting permission to enter Dar space," I said, mustering all the confidence I could.

"Hold your position," the person responded.

I did as told, idling down the engines and putting the shuttle into a holding pattern.

They responded soon. "Your request is denied. Turn around, or you will be fired upon."

That wasn't promising but also wasn't unexpected.

"There is no disrespect intended, but I'm unable to turn around," I said. *Here goes nothing.* "This shuttle will not hold together much longer. It's antiquated but all I had at my disposal. Please, I request sanctuary amongst my people."

Asking for sanctuary was a major card to lay down, and if it didn't pan out, I wasn't entirely sure what to try next. From everything I'd read, if sanctuary was requested, it couldn't be denied. But that little cultural tidbit was in a report from over five years before. Dar's restrictions had only grown tighter since then. I didn't know if the request would be honored.

When I didn't receive an immediate response, I felt the weight of my stupidity press down on me.

"*Jhan B-133*, your ship was ordered to alter course. Why have you refused our directives?" a new speaker asked.

"Please, I beg forgiveness. The ship's captain was going to comply with your orders, but I couldn't give up on my one chance to return home," I pleaded. I was regretting the whole idea.

"*Jhan B-133*, the order has been given. You must turn—" The comms went silent.

I panicked and checked everything I could think of. Everything was in working order, but the shuttle was old, and my plea about it falling apart at any moment wasn't a joke.

In desperation, I added, "I'm begging for your forgiveness. Please. I must be allowed to go to Dar. My husband's life depends upon it."

Silly, outrageous, dumb, stupid. I could've gone on. But Darquets were fiercely protective of their families. At least, those who colored inside the lines and married only full-blooded Darquets. Besides, a lie was best believed when partnered with the truth.

"*Jhan B-133*, you've crossed over into Darquet-controlled space. We will fire in thirty seconds if you do not alter course. Repeat, you will be fired upon if you—"

Sam, I'm going to need—

"*Jhan B-133*, orders have changed. You're cleared to continue. Please proceed on your present course. We will send a ship to intercept."

I breathed an enormous sigh of relief.

[Please repeat.]

Nothing. False alarm. I'll contact you later.

Docking with the Dar-controlled vessel didn't take long, nor was it particularly hard. *Thanks for teaching me the basics, Pops.* As soon as I thought that, I felt irritated with myself. I still didn't want to move away from the anger and betrayal I was harboring even though he'd done many things right as a father.

Pushing that irritation aside, I powered down the engines, stood, and moved to the rear hatch. That wasn't the time to be thinking about my father or my brother and the Orion family legacy. Right then, I was of Dar, and securing a heart stone was where my focus needed to be.

The pantsuit I'd chosen had an attached hood, and I brought it up until the edge rested just behind my hairline. The elbow-length sleeves showed off my newly elongated fingers, and the ankle-length pant legs revealed the newly minted gold sandals I'd chosen, which paired nicely with the scales covering my feet and winding up my legs.

My heart pounded, and my stomach threatened to revolt, but I brought my hands in front of my eyes, with the edges of my pinkie fingers touching. I leaned forward slightly and kept my gaze on the floor, no matter how tempted I was to look up as the shuttle door opened. Whatever had happened on their end to change their mind and allow me to dock, I didn't want to blow it with a rude greeting posture.

I sensed nothing but silence until a gentle breeze teased the edges of the hood and caressed my hands and face. When my lungs felt as if they were going to burst, I exhaled and sucked in a deep breath. The smell certainly wasn't what I was expecting—no hint of the faint metallic or stale air produced by scrubbers. Instead, I picked up delicate floral notes cut with a deeper and headier smell I couldn't place.

"Rise and take your place amongst your people, child of Dar, keeper of the sacred trust," someone intoned.

As I bowed, I moved my right hand between my left hand and face to touch my left shoulder, and as I straightened, I moved my left hand to touch my right shoulder. When my eyes hit the steady gaze of the Darquet standing before me, I lowered both of my hands, palms facing outward, to my sides.

"Honor and respect are given upon your lineage. To all who have come before you and all who come after you," I said then bowed once more and interlaced my fingers and let my hands rest in front of me.

"You are welcome, child of Dar," the man said.

A part of me wanted to relax, but I couldn't. Welcoming platitudes didn't mean nothing dangerous or insidious were behind them.

"Have you long been gone from the embrace of Dar?" he asked.

"I must carry my apologies upon the winds. I have yet to set foot on Dar," I replied.

The man held out a hand, and with my left one, I accepted his offer of polite support as I moved out of the shuttle and stepped into a ship I never could've imagined.

I knew of rumors, memories of a time when a select few had been invited to travel or tour an *eri vata ormt*. Even with all the linguistic experts and AI programs, no adequate translation could explain what that type of ship was. All anyone could do was refer to it as a Ship of Dar. While that wasn't the best linguistically, it was in fact a literal idea of what that type of ship had been built to represent. No matter the class—warship, transport, or personnel craft—the eri vata ormt could become anything they wanted.

They were oval-shaped behemoths, capable of sustaining an entire ecosystem inside. Instead of the cold metallic floors of conventional ships, soil was the surface I stood on—rich, dark, fertile soil. Off to my right stretched an endless meadow of luscious green grass, and to my left rose a great forest of beautiful purple-and-blue-leafed trees. Not a hint of anything artificial was in sight. I didn't know how the illusion of an endless horizon had been crafted. My brain knew walls had to be somewhere, but I couldn't find them.

As the Darquet led me away from the shuttle, I twisted, expecting to see the hangar door I'd flown through, but the aperture was gone, and to my horror, so was the shuttle.

"You must not fret, child of Dar. This is the way, to leave behind the taint of those forever mourning to be bereft of the beauty of our world," the man said.

I didn't know about mourning over something I'd never seen before, but I was certainly going to mourn over the loss of the shuttle. It'd been a backup plan in case I needed to make a hasty exit—as quick an exit as a shuttle of its age could, anyway. But it'd still been something. Suddenly, I had nothing but my own wits to survive my little jaunt to Dar.

Well, there is one more thing.

Those stupid smart-bots and their cursed timing—they popped up to interrupt just when the plot started boiling.

I slipped through the brilliant shafts of light more easily than before. The smells, sounds, and cares of the physical world fell away without a second thought. Warm light moved across my skin, and I let my head fall back as I soaked up the delicious rays of light.

The experience was intoxicating, more so than the other times, and before I lost complete control, I experienced a moment of knowing I was in danger of getting lost in the beauty of it all. But as soon as my subconscious rang the alarm bell, it was silenced, and I closed my eyes, sinking into the light's embrace.

9

Never Alone

My perception of time had gone, but eventually my eyelids fluttered open and I was aware I wasn't alone. I felt no fear or concern. Instead, I instinctively knew the presence I sensed was necessary and most welcome. The sunlight had felt complete, whole, and peaceful, but as the presence slipped in between those delicious rays of light, a new understanding dawned. I was not yet fully whole. A piece was missing.

My awareness shifted to a tendril of shadow. *No, that's wrong.* It wasn't shadow but merely an absence of light. I'd understood that once before but had forgotten.

The darkness flowed forward until it wrapped me half in light and half in its absence. Along the edge of the two, I could feel an inquisitiveness, as though two individuals were meeting for the first time, unafraid and curious about the other, each seeking the possibilities of what was to come.

As I allowed the sensations to wash over me, the understanding that something was incomplete took over as the dominant feeling. The peace I'd felt crumbled, but I resisted and tried to hold on. For the first time, I felt pain as I refused to yield, mild and just beneath the surface.

No, that isn't right. Not missing. Lost. Or broken. Or perhaps even stolen.

What am I supposed to do?

I threw the question out as the discomfort drew a part of me back to reality. And as I fought to remain in the sensations, I got a reply—not in words, but only the impression of something trying to break through, trying to communicate. Whatever it was, was asking for help.

How can I help when I don't understand?

Pain settled in the center of my chest, and it snatched away the light and the darkness. Confused and unsettled, I couldn't stop the terrified scream that ripped through me. I probably sounded like a depressurization alarm.

But through the echoes of my scream, a soothing voice was whispering to me. I couldn't make out the words even as I strained to hear them.

Up on the top of an Eternal Tower on one of the lunar bases, the pressure makes people's ears feel blocked, and all the surrounding sounds diminish. Then if someone gets pushed off the top of the tower, they fall down to the ground, and their ears pop, and suddenly, they can hear everything again, as clear as day.

That was how it felt.

"Breathe deep," a voice chanted.

I tried and struggled. A putrid smell coated the

insides of my nostrils and trickled its way down my throat. My fingers clawed at my mouth and nose as I tried to dislodge the obstruction, but two firm hands wrapped around my wrists and held them down at my sides. I twisted and turned and tried to break free. A panic attack was quickly on the rise.

"Breathe, just breathe," someone else said, startling me out of my panic attack.

My eyes opened wide, and I looked down at the hands holding me. I slowly lifted my gaze to stare into the amber eyes of Cain. Even with the added cranial ridges flushing out his Darquet ancestry, I knew to whom those eyes belonged.

I tried to take a deep breath and gagged at the putrid smell, but that time, my airways cleared, and my next breath was full and deep and unobstructed. Mercifully, the nasty odor was gone too.

"You must rest now and find the peace within, young one," said the first person who'd spoken.

While I didn't want to tear my gaze away from Cain, curiosity won out. I turned my head and caught sight of an ancient female Darquet. Her skin was lined with wrinkles, which obscured strange tattoo-like markings along her cheeks. The ashen-colored hair so famous among Darquets had turned completely black with age and was cut short.

"There is time for instruction and understanding yet, but you must first rest," she said. "Because of your long journey and most unusual circumstances, we will allow your husband to remain at your side until we are sure your health has been restored."

She gave me a small nod, turned, and leaned on a large cane as she left the room.

Surely, I'm dreaming. I would've pinched myself to make sure, but Cain still had a hold of my wrists.

"I feel like I'm missing a part of the story here," I said and was surprised to hear how raspy my voice sounded.

Cain squeezed my wrists then slowly let his hands slip away. The amber faded from his eyes, to violet, as he watched me.

"I'm waiting," I said. "What in Saturn's rings are you doing here? How? When I left, you were starting recovery."

Oh, those eyes. Such an unguarded window. The edges of his irises shimmered emerald and hinted at something even deeper and darker.

"I'm here because you rushed into a situation you don't understand," he growled. Then he stood. "The *Samaritan* was contacted about your... condition, and Sam confirmed your biosigns were erratic. Something had to be done."

I grinned. I couldn't help it. My Cain was there, my Mr. Surly Grumpy Face. And I thought that he, in good old-fashioned Cain tradition, would march over to the door, fling it open, and leave. But he didn't. He couldn't. Cain struggled to move, with an odd shuffle to his gait, and I realized he must've been in a great deal of pain.

No tears. I won't cry. Stop it.

But the reaction was involuntary. Watching him struggle hurt. I scrubbed the tears away before he could see and tried to think of something else, anything else to take my mind off knowing how much the IGJ had taken from him, how much his loyalty to me had cost him.

Cain made it to the door, but instead of opening it, he pressed an ear up against it. He stood there for a few moments before he appeared satisfied and made his way back to the extravagant bed then sat down on the edge.

"For once, Miles and I agreed about something. You were stupid to leave like you did. Your actions put everything in jeopardy. Not only your life, but mine and everyone who'd worked so hard to set this whole thing up," he said.

"What was I supposed to do? Sit around and watch you suffer? I came here in order to help you. I left the way I did because I care about you, you insufferable man," I huffed.

Cain pulled back his lip and snarled. "I know that."

"Then what?"

"Keep your voice down. Yelling will only draw their attention," Cain said.

I clenched my jaw and crossed my arms tight against my chest. "Would you kindly make sense, please? Did the IGJ rattle some of your brain cells?"

Whoops. As soon as the words left my mouth, I felt horrible. The good old Mahia was shining through.

"I'm sorry. I didn't mean that. I'm just... well, what—" I stopped. *Why dig a hole?*

To his credit, Cain didn't pull away or appear to grow any more upset with me than he already was.

"You shouldn't have left before Dr. Kell had a chance to do something about those smart-bots," Cain said in a clipped tone. "And you should have told me, or at least someone, what was going on. We could have prevented all of this."

"All of what? Told you what?" I was genuinely confused.

Cain leaned forward and lowered his voice. "Miles told me what he did." Pure rage flashed on his face. "About injecting the smart-bots. But in true Miles fashion, he didn't offer a lot of details, only that the Star Eaters were supposed to give you some kind of choice or options."

"What does that have to do with anything?" I asked.

A hint of emerald crept into his eyes. "How long have you been on Dar?"

I pushed myself up and stared at him. "I don't know. Maybe twelve hours or fewer? I docked with the ship... Wait, we're on Dar?"

Cain nodded. "So how much time do you think has passed?"

I didn't like where his question was going. I flung the covers back and scooted out of bed. As I tried to stalk past him, Cain reached out and grabbed my arm. Even as weak as he was, he could still pull me back down.

"How much time?" he growled.

"I don't know. If we're on Dar, twenty-four hours?"

"Wrong. You've been on Dar for over a week."

10

Trust Issues

I stared at him then busted out laughing. "Nice try."

When he didn't drop the act and join me in laughing at his silly joke, I snapped my mouth shut.

"After what the Ascended described happened, it's not surprising you don't realize how much time has passed." He leaned forward and whispered. "How do you think I'm able to be here? I wouldn't have been welcome on Dar without some… adjustments."

He was right. Logically, I knew he was. When I'd left Cain, he couldn't get out of bed. After he'd spent so much time in a coma, Dr. Kell would've insisted on stabilizers and regrowth boosters, and even with such advanced drugs, Cain would've needed at least a few days to allow his body time to adjust—not to mention the gene-mods for passing any purity tests the Darquets might demand. No way could he have received those treatments, been able to get up and move around, then travel to Dar in twenty-four hours, give or take. *But a week?*

"What about the crew? Miles? Lio?" I asked.

Cain clenched his jaw. "Waiting. Barely. Your little

escapade hasn't earned you points among most of the crew. But Lio and Miles are standing firm. For now."

"Lio is?" I was pleased to know I'd made a new friend. *An entire week. Had there been more to the vision than what I remembered? How could I have zoned out for so long?*

"Mahia, why didn't you tell them what was happening to you?" he asked. That time, he showed no hint of anger or annoyance, just pure concern.

"I don't know what you're talking about," I said. I was lying. I knew I just didn't want to say it out loud, which was strange because I'd been waiting for Cain to wake up so that I could talk to someone I trusted. But when the moment arrived, the words got stuck in my throat.

I shook my head. "Don't worry about me. What about you?"

Cain stiffened and pulled back. "I'll be fine. Right now, we need to understand what's going on with you."

Two could play that game. "You first," I insisted. "You refused to speak to me. Jumping Jupiters, you didn't even want to see me when you woke up. Now you're here, all eager and ready to help?"

Cain turned away. "What would you know of it?"

The little self-control I'd mustered snapped. "Excuse me? Do you have a homicidal brother on the loose, destroying worlds? Or tricked into carrying the same thing that was inside Triton and all those other fools my father killed on the *Rapscallion*?"

"Keep your voice down."

"Don't tell me what to do," I hissed. "I was waiting for you, hoping every day you would wake up and I would have someone to confide in, someone I could trust to talk to, to work out this messed-up little puzzle with. I thought we were on the same team."

I watched Cain struggle for a response. I should've backed down. We'd both been through hell on the *Justus* in different ways.

But I didn't. "Should I have an arm or a leg cut off? Would that make us even?"

Cain turned his head to stare at me. The violet deepened to the blackest of nights. He lunged forward and pinned me to the bed. "Don't you ever say something like that again. Do you hear me?"

I should've been afraid. I'd seen what Cain was capable of in those moments. And underneath my hurt and fear, I knew the horror of the emotional-physical wringer he'd been through. *How deep does his damage go?*

But I wasn't afraid—irritated and scared, sure, as I'd taken a chance to open myself up and had been unprepared to cope with needing to give support instead of simply taking it.

I broke free and knocked Cain onto his back. I scrambled out of the bed and stood there, staring at him as he stared back.

I was in the wrong, unable to outmaneuver my own acid tongue. <*I'm sorry. I shouldn't have… but this is… We're complicated. And I don't know how to…*>

That wasn't a great apology. It probably shouldn't have been considered an apology but a stupid, stammering attempt at trying to back my way out of what I'd said.

The black receded from his eyes, but he didn't turn away.

<*I guess I've still got a lot of work to do, huh? Maybe there's*

a class or something I can take. Or a bioupgrade that'll stop me from saying stupid stuff like that.>

I tried to make light of the situation, but when Cain didn't respond, not even a twitch of a muscle, I frowned.

"Did you hear what I said?"

He blinked, and that time, he turned away.

That was the crux of the matter. It wasn't the physical torture or losing his tail but the damage done to the telepathic link between us. I should have realized it sooner. While I didn't understand the implications of being heart's blood, I knew it was deeply important to Cain.

I sat down on the bed and pushed myself back against the ornate headboard. "Can you hear me?"

"Yes."

I paused. "But you can't respond."

"Yes."

"When I get a heart stone, we'll fix it. I'll fix it."

Cain rolled over and stared at me. "There is no fixing this. My family's heart stone was destroyed, remember?"

"I know. But there has to be a way." And I meant it.

I couldn't do much about what was going on in the larger scope of the known worlds, but what was going on between us was something I could try to fix. If the heart stones held the ability to heal—and I mean everything from physical to emotional to mental—then I would figure out their secret and snag a new heart stone for Cain and his family. And if I couldn't find the answers on Dar, then I would look elsewhere. *Perhaps when I'm able to talk with the Master of Dentar, he'll have some answers.*

"I'm not giving up. Not on you, and not on…" I swallowed. "Not on us."

Cain struggled but pulled himself up next to me. The amount of effort it took concerned me, but I decided that wasn't the time to comment.

"I'm not entirely sure I'm worth the effort," he whispered.

"Excuse me?"

"I'm not… what you think. There's a lot you don't know about me, and—"

I turned and reached out to gently touch his cheek. "We all come with pasts, don't we? I mean, don't forget my family name, right?"

Cain snorted. "Right."

"You said we would try to trust each other."

He nodded.

"Then let's keep trying. I know we didn't get off to a great start before, with the horrid interruption by the commandant and all that, but we can try again."

Mushiness—situations and emotions I'd worked hard to avoid in my life. And believe me, I've got a long way to go, but for Cain, I would let a little of those squishy, feel-good emotions creep through.

"I really am sorry. I don't know why my mouth runs off like—"

Cain leaned forward and kissed me, light and soft.

"I happen to like your mouth," he murmured.

I blushed the deepest red imaginable. "Right, well…"

He smirked, a delicious smirk that would haunt my dreams.

"So…"

He grinned. "So. Back to my question. Why didn't you at least talk to Dr. Kell about the seizures and the blackouts? I understand a reluctance to talk to Miles, but you should've at least alerted her about what had happened."

I sighed. "I know, and I don't know. I wanted to talk to you first. I mean, talking to her about it would open up a caseload of nasty zips. What if she had too many questions that would lead to my father and what he did? That's not common knowledge, at least not yet, anyway."

"Fair enough."

I was glad he didn't pressure me. "Wait. You would have seen me, wouldn't you?"

Cain blinked in surprise at the question. "Seen you?"

"What I was having… the blackout or whatever. Is that what it really looked like? Some type of seizure?"

His eyes narrowed, and he regarded me with a suspicious look. "Mahia."

I frowned and hesitated. *You promised to trust each other. This is a chance to try. You have to at least try.*

After a deep breath, I said, "I don't black out. I think I… go somewhere? I'm bathed in light, and—"

The door to the room burst open, and a very tall, very irate-looking female Darquet stood in the doorway.

"Announce yourself," she commanded.

I stared at her in confusion and glanced at Cain as he hastily got to his feet. When I didn't move with him, he reached down and pulled me up to stand next to him.

"Forgive us, Holy One. We've only heard rumors

but are unaccustomed to being in the presence of one such as yourself," Cain said.

"Pointless drivel. Announce yourself," she said.

"I am Iim ed-Eim, and this is my wife, Serea el-Merea ed-Taom, Holy One," Cain said. He raised his hands in the gesture of greeting and supplication as I hurried to follow suit.

"As expected. Lineages we're unfamiliar with," she said with a sniff. "You, daughter of Dar, shall come with us."

"I must beg forgiveness, please, Holy One," Cain said with a second gesture of supplication. "May I first finish the exchange of greetings and health with my wife?"

"We're pressed for time, but I am told an exception in this case will yield results. Do so, quickly."

That wasn't the most gracious of gestures, that's for sure.

Cain turned and pulled me close, his lips close to my ears. "You foolish woman. Whatever those smart-bots have done to you, they mimic the trances the Holy Ones experience. Now, they think you're one of them. Play into your ignorance of never having been to Dar and having been so far removed from Darquets. Get them to answer your questions without giving them answers to theirs. If they think you are a false Holy One, we'll both be put to death."

11

Dar

Well. Damn.

I was a tad bit upset and unsure of what in the world had been going on—probably how Pluto felt, being tossed back and forth from planet land to plutoidville.

Those reports Miles and Dr. Ashter had provided didn't include any information on this sudden development—nothing about Holy Ones or anything hinting of another major player besides the Ruling Council. This was kind of a major deal, especially when death was on the table.

"Trances? I'm mimicking the... What now?" I whispered, as things clicked into place. My irritation at the lack of information was gone. I'd finally landed in a place that could provide answers. And if this "Holy One" wasn't forthcoming, too bad.

"Just listen," Cain growled. "Ascended and Holy Ones may request their husband join them if they are married or have been promised before being accepted into the Halls. But that's a place I can't go—only females are allowed there—yet you can request I be allowed to stay in your rooms. Do it. Now."

He pulled away, and for a moment—just a moment, mind you—I was tempted to pull him back and stay wrapped in his arms, to feel his solid warmth, to know he was going to be okay after seeing him so lifeless for so long in the medical bay.

A look of annoyance was in his eyes. He didn't need telepathy to know what I was thinking.

I turned to face the Holy One. *Eye contact or no eye contact?* With one glance at the fierce gaze, I decided on no eye contact.

"I would request my husband be allowed to remain within my rooms," I said in a demure voice.

The Holy One took in a sharp breath. "The laws of Dar must be obeyed. We are nothing without our laws."

When no further reply came, I sneaked a glance. I shouldn't have done that. I thought I was going to have nightmares about her. Whatever beauty had been etched on her face was gone, as in horror-story gone. Her irises and pupils had turned as white as the sclera, and where her pale skin showed off her veins, a fungus appeared to be spreading. Her head was tilted to one side as though listening to something only she could hear.

I couldn't tear my eyes away, like a classic prey-and-predator standoff in which the prey knows they've been caught and cannot escape.

The Holy One's unnerving gaze kept mine, and a haze of light appeared to surround her. I watched, enthralled and anticipating a grisly demise. The light brightened then went supernova.

I flung up my arm to shield my eyes and couldn't stop a small cry of surprise.

Immediately, I felt an arm around my shoulders, and Cain pulled me close, tucking me up against his side.

"She's still unwell. My wife needs time to rest and recover," Cain said with more defiance in his words than was healthy for either of us at the moment.

My arm dropped, and relief flooded me as the Holy One appeared normal again.

Her haughty expression of irritation shifted, and she laughed—not a charming laugh, but a full-on belly-deep peal of laughter.

"They believe the two of you shall provide an interesting divergence of time, although I have voiced my concerns. Iim ed-Eim, you shall remain here as I will not allow a threat to Dar to freely access our cities. And you, daughter of Dar, shall come with us," the Holy One said.

With a flourish, she turned and moved from the doorway. I looked at Cain, but he shook his head and gave me a push in her direction. I didn't need the push—I just wanted to make sure he was going to be okay. The last time we were separated, things hadn't ended up so swell. So I winked, and he scowled. *Great, we're on the same page again.*

Like a moth to a flame, I followed the Holy One out into the wide world of Dar. Well, not quite like a moth. I didn't plan on getting close enough to be singed. But I followed and intertwined my fingers, holding them at chest height as I walked out of the room, then I nearly had a heart attack.

Considering all the time I'd spent reading the reports, I should've been ready for it.

Dar architecture was hailed as a wonder, and despite the strict rules governing access to the world, engineers and designers on far-flung worlds still worked to mimic the splendor of Dar. Those who'd been to Dar before the lockdown always said no one ever came close. I seconded that opinion.

Darquets believed in maintaining unobstructed views of the land through a unique combination of ideas and styles. Buildings or structures that were required to be physically on the ground were carefully designed to blend into the natural environment with unique camouflaging flourishes, having as little environmental impact as possible. The majority of Darquet buildings weren't on land, though.

Residential areas, grand open-air theaters, and commercial needs were suspended in the sky. Heroic feats of engineering and nongravitational fields allowed the Darquets to live among the clouds. When Dar had been open to the known worlds, their unique way of living had made Dar the vacation hot spot—not only for the views and ethereal feels one could rake in, but for the sheer novelty of walking on air.

I would indeed get my answers even if that meant following the Holy One off the edge of the building.

According to what I'd read, the nongravitational fields stretched out around each physical building for a good five meters. Between structures, a series of nongrav bots suspended the fields, essentially creating bridges and walkways to connect the buildings. But the old tourist brochure warnings had been clear—if someone didn't pay attention to where they were going, they could easily walk right off the edge and experience a glorious, life-changing free fall.

I couldn't help but wonder how Dar children survived into adulthood.

The Holy One didn't bother to provide instruction, so I walked exactly where she had stepped. *Good thing I don't have a fear of heights.*

I glanced back at the building we'd exited. It wasn't large by any means and had a strange octagonal shape. I caught sight of similar pods farther down and surmised they must have been living quarters for somebody—I wasn't really sure who. *What did Cain say? The Ascended?*

When I turned my focus back in the direction we were headed, an enormous structure was in front of us with two smaller yet identical buildings on either side. Those had the same octagonal look as the pods, but on a larger scale and with several twisting spires reaching up through the clouds. As we grew closer, the natural light danced off the mirrorlike surfaces and threw a myriad of sun dogs into the air. It was breathtaking.

Fascinated, I asked, "What do you do about severe weather? How do you protect yourself or your buildings?"

The Holy One threw me a sour look. "Do you think we would not protect ourselves?"

"Of course. My apologies." *Keep it together. Remember who you're pretending to be.* "I'm merely overwhelmed by the beauty of our people. I haven't seen this type of architectural marvel elsewhere."

"You've been sheltered for too long," the Holy One

replied. "But rest assured. In emergencies, we have shielding and stabilizers embedded in each of the buildings. If a truly severe storm should occur, the buildings are programmed to come unattached from the moorings and ride out the storm. When the weather has calmed, the buildings are towed back into their designated locations. Or if a new arrangement is agreeable, then alterations are made."

I wasn't sure I was keen on the idea of riding out a major storm in a free-floating building, but the Darquets had maintained their technology for generations, and they were still quite populous. *Their casualty rate must be low.* That was encouraging.

When we were only a few meters from the largest of the three buildings, one of the mirror panels faded, and several female Darquets made their way toward us. They positioned themselves on either side of the invisible walkway and took up postures of supplication.

I swore I could feel more than a few unhappy looks as we passed. But no one stopped me, and I followed her into the structure, blinking in surprise. I'd expected a bright, airy interior, perhaps jeweled surfaces or more mirrors suspended in the air, maybe with a few crystal chandeliers or some such blingy madness thrown in.

But the interior was pitch black.

I stumbled and involuntarily reached out for support, only to snag my fingers in silky cloth.

The Holy One's voice echoed through the darkness. "True sight takes time. But fear it, for it may still come."

I regained my balance and blinked, hoping my eyes would adjust. Improved eyesight in the dark was supposed to have been one change from the gene-mods. With my luck, I would've gotten faulty gene-mods.

With the sea of darkness surrounding me, I decided my best bet was to stand still. *Who knows if the trickery of see-through walkways extends into a place like this?* I wasn't about to find out.

"State your lineage," the Holy One said.

After a deep breath and slow exhalation to calm my nerves, I replied. "I am Serea el-Merea ed-Taom, edtal-Kaom ed-Paom."

A thin shaft of light pierced the darkness off to my right. Small motes of dust seemed to be drifting in the beam, but as I watched, the particles stretched and thinned until they formed an intricate web. Images appeared, blurry at first but quickly growing sharp as they hung like dewdrops from the lines of the web.

The files I'd studied had included pictures of my supposed grandfather, Kaom ed-Paom, and his father as well. So, unfortunately, I recognized what the web was showing me. I knew Dar kept meticulous records of family lineages, but I had no idea they would be that detailed. At least twenty generations of images had to be there, swaying in a gentle breeze that didn't reach me.

I'm going to be lucky if they believe my story, I thought. The whole situation had been a tremendous gamble, one I'd already lost since I hadn't disclosed everything. Perhaps if I'd been honest with Dr. Kell, Miles or Dr. Ashter would've said something and nixed the entire plan because it teetered dangerously close to one of these so-called Holy Ones. Or maybe even they wouldn't have known what she was.

I held my breath as I watched the web and prayed no faces would appear below the Darquet who was supposed to be my grandfather. But blast it all out an airlock, a face appeared then another and another—three male faces. I swore they all turned their eyes toward me and glared. I didn't know what I would do if everything went sideways. *Can I take the Holy One hostage or fight my way back to Cain?*

Then another row of faces appeared and another and another. My chances of fooling anyone about who I was weren't looking good. In fact, I was pretty sure everything had taken a horrible, nasty turn. *Time for plan B. Or F.*

"Hold still," the Holy One intoned.

That was the last thing I was going to do. Nope, I needed to turn and run. Nothing good ever came after words like that. *How many women were there? We walked straight through the door and stopped. If I pivot and run straight back, maybe I can just smash my way through the building.*

"Ow!" I yelped, and my hand flew to the back of my neck. Something had bitten me. My skin burned as I touched the spot. "What was that?"

"Confirmation," the Holy One replied.

Off to my left, another shaft of light appeared, along with another spidery web of faces, images of people I knew.

Wats Hawking Orion.

Lucas Orion.

Mahia Orion.

The whole damned Orion family tree.

So much for running.

12

Trusting the Universe

Stating my case and throwing myself upon her mercy was the only option.

"You got me. But I'm here for good reason. My husband? Well, he's not actually my husband but my heart's blood, in fact. Crazy, right? But I'm here because Cain needs help. He was severely injured, well, tortured if we want to get into the nitty-gritty of it all. And it's all my fault he got caught up in some crazy—"

"Silence," the Holy One said.

The shafts of webbed light flared to life until they illuminated the entire space. I squinted and blinked at the change in lighting, and my gaze settled on the Holy One, bent slightly at the waist and listening to the furtive whispers of another female Darquet. *Had she always been there, waiting in the dark?* That was a sobering thought as I hadn't completely abandoned the run-for-it scenario.

The room was spacious, far larger than I would've guessed, and all one room. Putting the pieces together from what I'd studied, the importance of lineage, the title of Holy One, and the theatrics of displaying the fake and real lineages, I was leaning toward the theory that Darquets held a religious outlook on bloodlines.

That meant I'd probably committed a mortal sin or whatever they labeled that type of deceit. I had a sinking feeling as the Holy One nodded her head a few times then turned to look at me. Our entire setup had been a tad bit arrogant—to think we could fool a highly advanced species into believing I was a full-blooded Darquet. *Humanity's hubris, perhaps? Or just the folly of people who felt there weren't any other options?*

Whatever it was, I didn't have any weapon to defend myself, and the room certainly held nothing I could grab.

Well, I guess I'm going to get to experience skydiving. Yay, me.

The Holy One straightened, and the other Darquet hurriedly moved past me, but I didn't dare turn my back on the Holy One to see where or how the other one exited the room—not yet.

"I take full responsibility for breaking the laws and coming to Dar. But I couldn't sit idly by and watch Cain die… or worse. All I need is access to a heart stone. Key it in to his biology, or whatever it is that you do, and just wait for however long it takes the rock to complete its mojo and heal him." I took a quick breath and let the words rush out: "Then also negotiate the release of his sister."

Why not just cram the whole encheala into one fluffy bean-curd wrap? A scrumptious Telt food mash-up, if I do say so myself.

I was certain Cain hadn't forgotten about her and was no doubt running through plans while he waited for me. Then the nasty little voice had to rear its head: *Did Cain really come here for me? Or was he so close to Dar he'd come for his sister?* I still had a slew of my own issues to continue working through.

"Heart's blood does not abandon heart's blood," the Holy One quipped.

I stared at her, and I was ashamed to admit that my mouth dropped open too. *There's no way she could have heard me. Must be some cryptic proverb or something.*

"In certain circumstances, it can teach the young. But for now, it should at least answer your immediate concern," she said.

My jaw hit the floor. "Great. You're all telepathic?"

"No, not all," the Holy One said. She turned and beckoned me to follow.

The time had come to choose—run and take a chance or follow her and see where it led. But my pesky sense of curiosity took over, and I was determined to get some answers.

We moved through the space in silence until we reached the other side of the building. The Holy One stopped, and when she made the motion to sit down—on thin air—a chair abruptly sprang into form. From her expression, I figured she expected me to follow suit, and I did, just waiting to fall, but I fell into a rather comfortable chair. *Nifty.*

"Indeed, it is," she said with a slight smirk.

"So," I said and glanced around. "Death? Life?"

"Perhaps."

Great, another cryptic school graduate. Is the universe just lining them up for me or what?

The Holy One settled back in the chair and stared at me. "It shall all depend upon what we find."

I didn't like the sound of that but remembered Cain's suggestion of playing into ignorance in order to gain answers. But I suspected that wouldn't go down well with this Darquet.

"I really apologize, but I'm not sure what you want from me," I said.

"That's quite apparent, but they shall see what they shall see. Then we'll consider the male," the Holy One replied. She lifted a hand and held it in midair, and a small wooden cup appeared, with wisps of steam coming from the liquid inside.

I sat up a little more, truly intrigued. That was seriously advanced tech, a level I'd never seen or read about.

"Upon scanning your vessel, we knew you were human and were working to manipulate our beliefs for your own gain. But with closer inspection, our scans revealed the possibility you may be able to manifest the *quorm ra dath*. At first, we believed you carried a touch of Darquet within your blood, but it is clear you do not. Nor does it appear you carry a spark of life within your belly, which could have accounted for an occurrence." She took a small sip of her drink.

I couldn't help but blush at her implications. "No, I'm not pregnant."

She nodded and set the cup on a small table that appeared next to her chair.

"No. The lineage markers would have indicated another generation. So we wonder how is it you manifest the *quorm ra dath*? What is it that gives you this unique ability?"

While I wasn't familiar with the words she was using,

I knew what she was talking about. And I struggled with how to answer her question. My intuition told me to tell her the truth. To do otherwise would not only be a grave insult to her position, potentially shutting the door on any help for Cain and his sister, but I was also getting the distinct impression the Holy One didn't care for me all that much. I wondered if confessing all would score some brownie points.

If I told her about the smart-bots and the Star Eaters, I would surrender a gigantic piece of information that could be later used against me—or Cain or even Miles. I wasn't sure I was actually too concerned about Miles, but I did see a certain wisdom in hedging my bets and keeping a little bit to myself.

This is crazy, I thought before I caught myself. But the Holy One merely quirked an eyebrow and patiently waited for my response.

I closed my eyes for a moment to block out everything else as I considered my options. At that critical juncture in the whole messed-up ordeal, I wasn't sure which road would lead to the smallest number of scars. I highly doubted I could finish that whole crazy journey without more than a few bumps and bruises.

I remembered what I'd witnessed—the light, the darkness, and the certainty something else was there, aware and watching. And not just watching but asking for help about something that had been lost or perhaps broken.

Alright. Time for a leap of faith. I needed answers, and if the universe had decided to lend a helping hand for once, then I was going to take it, but not without a few questions of my own. *I mean, fair is fair.*

"Everyone seems to want something from me. So what is it you want?" I asked.

The Holy One's gaze never left my face as she reached for her cup, took a sip, then set it back down. "The truth. And by that truth, you and the male shall be judged."

"Back to the life or death, then," I said.

"Those concepts would depend upon your perception and understanding of each word, but that is a discussion for a different time," she responded.

Frustration bubbled over, and I stood. "All I want are some straight answers without a tangled mess of wordplay to stumble over. Do you think you can do that?"

The Holy One blinked then nodded. "Yes. It is within my discretion." She stood and said, "Come."

"I thought you wanted me to tell you how I could manifest the *quorm ra dath*," I said.

"We do, but it has been considered. If you're given something of great importance, then perhaps you will feel more comfortable in doing so as well," she said as she turned and walked toward the wall, which vanished as she approached, revealing the bright blue sky.

Alright, universe, you'd better not be messing with me.

I could've sworn I heard her chuckle as we stepped outside.

13

The Spire of the Third

The magnitude of the building we left had obscured the view behind it when we'd entered from other side. Beyond the building and its two smaller companions was a breathtaking and awe-inspiring arrangement of floating platforms and buildings.

The platforms varied in size, but all were covered in thick, luscious vegetation. Forests and grasslands abounded, with a small mountain range on one, which appeared to have a lake surrounded by beautiful red-leafed trees. A few of the platforms even had birds riding the currents as they dipped and dived around the wispy tops of the vegetation.

The buildings were different shapes and configurations, but all sported some type of the mirror paneling, glinting in the bright light of day and casting more sun dogs. Between the platforms and buildings were smaller objects moving back and forth, and with a jolt of shock, I realized they were Darquets.

The Holy One stopped and turned. "Welcome to Dar. What you witness results from generations of ingenuity fueled by desperation, the need to protect our species, to ensure its survival."

I certainly hadn't been expecting that little speech. "Protection? From what, the purist movements?"

A look of sorrow crossed her face before she regained her composure. "No. We do not fear the weapons or machinations of those who deem interspecies relationships anathema."

"Yet even your own official reports stated you closed Dar to trade and tourism because of the rise of the purist movement. And, ironically, became your own type of purist ideology," I had to point out.

"Do you believe all the reports your government puts out? Should we be concerned about harboring two deadly criminals aligned with those who are destroying moons and stations and heavily populated habitats?"

"Excuse me?"

"According to the media, you and the male are wanted for questioning by the InterGalactic Justice system because of your potential involvement with the destruction of Lunar 5," the Holy One calmly stated. "I assume they will add on charges for Starbase 9.2 and Cloud-11 in time."

"We had nothing to do with that," I said. "It was my brother."

She tilted her head to the side, watching and silently judging me.

"No. No cryptic, mystic mumbo jumbo here. On this, we need to be crystal clear. Cain and I have nothing to do with what Lucas is doing. The IGJ is merely using the announcement as a front for their own twisted purposes," I snapped. "And if you think I'm just going to—"

The Holy One raised a hand. "We were merely trying to make a point. We know you and the male were not involved. Just because we closed our world to the outside doesn't mean we are ignorant of the events unfolding around us."

She reached out and tapped the air. Within a heartbeat, a small platform appeared, complete with guardrails and manicured grass.

"Come. I am being told it's time they made you aware," the Holy One said as she stepped up onto the platform. "But know this: If you break the laws of Dar, *I* will see to it they do not shield you from those consequences. Life on Dar is sacred and to be held in reverence. Our ways have shielded and protected us for generations. I will not let an outsider, out of mere curiosity, change what generations have set down before us."

"I understand," I said. And I did. I was walking a fine line, and I needed to keep my focus if I was going to get answers.

Attempting to not gape at the surrounding scenery, I fixed my gaze on a point in the distance as we moved through the sky. *Made aware of what? How the worlds are falling apart?* I knew chaos was growing out there. Governments were responding without understanding exactly who the enemy was. Citizens on dozens of worlds were fearful of being wiped out in a blink of an eye. I felt like I was stuck inside a jute-store horror novel, with my brother as the evil villain incarnate.

And the IGJ could get sucked into a black hole, for all I cared. Commandant Yilmaz should've been at the forefront of tracking down Lucas and his gang and working to coordinate with governments about coming together and defeating the enemy. That was what the organization was there for. Instead, Yilmaz was distracted and wasting her time worrying about what my father and his cronies had been up to.

By the time I'd run out of angry vitriol, I realized we were moving at a gentle downward angle. I glanced in the direction we were headed and saw a tall spire gracefully extending off the planet's surface and piercing the sky.

"What is that?" I asked.

"The Spire of the Third," the Holy One said with reverence. "Our most sacred place on Dar." Then, with more than a hint of annoyance, she added, "You should be most grateful. This is not for the eyes of the outside world."

I was in a xenologist's dream, invited into the inner sanctum of Darquet culture. Even when Dar was the go-to tourist hot spot, an air of mystery had surrounded the inner workings of Dar. That was one reason Dr. Ashter and other xenologists relished the chance to unravel those hidden aspects. Everyone wanted to know what was hiding behind the veil of beauty and wonder. *Is it something even more fantastical? Or will the curtain be pulled back to reveal a great disappointment?* That led me to wonder what my father had really wanted to study there. *He would relish being where I'm standing right now.*

"Yes. Wats Hawking Orion was a man of many faces, and despite his complex nature, he held a reverence for the beauty of other cultures and societies and how they express themselves," the Holy One said.

"What do you know about him?" I asked, unable to mask the bitterness in my voice. The question was rhetorical.

Everyone claimed to know my father, to understand his motivations. The media, the whisper nets, the IGJ, and even random strangers I would occasionally run into wanted to sit down and talk with me about him.

"We know his bid to spend time on Dar was rejected," she responded.

"What?" I whipped my head around to stare at her.

"Your father petitioned the Dar Ruling Council to spend time amongst the Ascended, to discuss the finer points of our religion and ties to the stars," she said with a neutral expression as she regarded me. "They normally pass those types of petitions to my acolytes, then they bring them to my attention. But the Ruling Council rejected his bid, ignoring centuries of tradition on the matter."

"It wasn't the Ruling Council. Dr. Sia-Ial Ashter rejected his bid," I said.

The Holy One's serene countenance slipped, and she snarled, revealing four very sharp canines. "Do not mention his name here, in this place."

I gaped and swallowed a couple of bugs too.

The fungus-like substance trailing along the Holy One's veins moved—literally moved, as in squirming and shifting position. It was no longer in thin lines mirroring the veins but fanned out into intricate patterns, twisting back and forth on each other.

I took a step back and bumped up against the guard-rail. With a glance, I tried to calculate how far down I'd fall if I jumped. *Would every bone in my body break? Probably.*

"You would not survive," she hissed. "That man is nothing more than a bloated piece of flesh. We should have suspected his hand in the matter. Selfishness and conceit cling to him."

"Are we talking about the same guy here?" I asked.

Dr. Ashter was indeed a little snobbish, but considering what he'd been able to accomplish in his extended life span, I would've been willing to cut the guy a few breaks.

"You would do far better to follow your father's example than the one of that man," the Holy One said as she tried to regain her composure.

I scoffed. "You've got to be kidding me. My father? Who murdered a slew of people? Who sided with the cloud-sucking Eeri? That man?"

"How woefully ignorant you are," she replied with a sad shake of her head. "But it was to be expected. We do not imply your father was a perfect man. He should have heeded my advice, following the way of Dar in affording his female offspring the opportunities instead of the male."

"Lady, I don't know who you've been listening to, but Lucas and our father didn't get along."

"From your perspective."

Great, we're back in cryptic land. "If you've got something to say, then do it. Otherwise, quit beating around the bush," I said.

The fungus shifted again into thin wavy lines, and

the Holy One smiled. "You will find the balance you seek, but only in time. Answers of the magnitude you seek must be revealed carefully, or the entire endeavor will rot from within."

Cain had advised me to remain cryptic in order to draw out answers without revealing too much. But I wasn't in the mood to play games.

"What if I don't want to be patient?"

"Then we shall see if your father died for nothing," the Holy One said as the platform came to a stop.

I stood there, unable to fully digest her statement. "Are you saying what my father did, he did for me?"

She inclined her head to one side. "Perhaps." The Holy One didn't indicate I was to follow her that time. She simply turned and walked toward the Spire of the Third.

Her response didn't make sense to me. *What was it that Miles had said… that he wasn't sure if the cosmos was playing some kind of joke on me? Sneaky little scuttle crab knew more than he let on. Typical.* I'd come to Dar as a side trip, a brief detour on the route to cosmic revelation land because I'd felt obligated—that wasn't the right word. Cain wasn't an obligation. Honestly, I'd come to Dar because I loved Cain. *There, done. Now to move on.* Yet the universe had seen fit to rear up and say, "Ha ha, sucker! Gotcha."

So be it. I was going to grab it by its scrawny little neck and—

The Holy One's voice drifted back to me. "There is no joke. Events have simply unfolded as they have. Whether guided by some unseen wind or merely through the impossible odds of you coming to this place when you need it most, we do not know."

Moments before, I'd been ready for the universe to cough up some answers. But those answers came with a hefty price tag. Apparently, I was about to confront some more ideas about my father. I wasn't entirely sure that was worth the price of admission.

On a serious note, though, I didn't know what I was really going to do. *Stand on the platform and pout? Stomp my feet and refuse to follow?* I didn't think so. I was an Orion, after all.

14

Into the Belly of the Beast

The Spire of the Third wasn't covered in the mirrorlike surface the other buildings boasted. Instead, it was coated with strips of dull silver that didn't reflect light but absorbed the sun's rays instead. The visual effect reminded me of what I'd felt in the darkness. The tall spire was the perfect embodiment of what I'd experienced during the visions. I struggled to wrap my mind around the concept.

I twisted around to look at the buildings above us, their mirrored surfaces twinkling like jewels in the sky, reflecting and refracting the bright light of the afternoon sun in glorious abandon. Warmth, peace, and beauty reflected in a corporeal manner. Opposite was the Spire of the Third, peaceful in its own right but cool, dark, and strangely inviting.

"Are you a Star Eater?" I asked.

The Holy One stopped and turned to face me. "No. Come."

That was disappointing, but all things considered, it

wasn't a ridiculous possibility. Nature loved to camouflage poisonous things with bright colors.

As we approached the spire, I was sure it must've had a handful of antigrav bots to ensure the whole thing didn't wilt like a lollipop flower on Ka Secondary. The base of the building had four arched supports on each corner, extending outward like the fingers of a giant hand reaching deep into the earth.

The Holy One ducked underneath an arch and vanished into the darkness, and I followed. My eyes adjusted, and at first glance, I believed the interior of the arch was covered in intricate patterns. But as my eyesight sharpened, I saw the patterns shift and realized it appeared to be made of the same substance covering the Holy One.

The Holy One moved to the center of the space beneath the arch, where a thin pillar rose from the ground and traveled up through the spire's interior. I squinted as I craned my neck to look up. The same strange fungal substance coated the pillar as well, and if my eyes weren't playing tricks on me, it looked as though it created an intricate web between the thin pillar and the interior spire walls.

"I don't like spiders," I muttered.

When I brought my attention back to the Holy One, her milky-white eyes sent a few shivers down my spine. "I am not convinced this is the way."

"Then what are we doing here?"

"There is no choice. Not without great sacrifice. Something we aren't willing to do."

Not exactly comforting.

Without preamble, the Holy One stretched out a hand, and her fingers brushed the central pillar. Despite the eerie horror vibes she was giving off, I was a lot more curious than afraid. I bet I could count on one hand the number of non-Darquets who'd witnessed that sacred space.

When her skin contacted the pillar, the funguslike substance on her body flowed across her skin, down her arm, and across the pillar. In a tangled web of intricate lines, it joined with what was on the central pillar, spinning itself into a thick circle. As it spun, adding new layers, it moved down until it rested on the ground. And through no means of technology I could even wrap my head around, a hole appeared in the ground.

"What you seek here will not provide all the answers you are looking for, but it will provide clarification… if you are worthy," the Holy One said as she stepped to one side.

"You're not coming?" I asked as she gestured toward the hole.

"What lies beneath is not for one such as I. I am merely a humble guardian, not a vessel."

"And how exactly does this help Cain?"

"If you are judged worthy, then so may he also be."

"I would prefer assurances first," I said as I took a step closer to stare down into the pit of doom. "If I'm not worthy, or whatever that means, Cain certainly is." I looked up at the Holy One. "He's a good person and deserves a chance to heal—physically, mentally, and emotionally. You guys keep the information about heart stones close to the chest, so I don't know how it all works, but I want your word you'll help him no matter what happens to me."

The Holy One tilted her head, and in a wide grin exposing her canines, she said, "I shall make an agreement with you, daughter of Wats Hawking Orion. If they judge you unworthy, then I shall see to it personally that Turen ed-Suren is placed with the heart stones." She looked away. "No more shall be said on the matter."

"Thanks." I bowed in supplication. "So how does this work exactly?"

"Step forward in faith, and faith shall see you through."

I wasn't going to waste time getting into a philosophical wormhole over faith, so I took a deep breath and stepped into darkness.

And I found no solid ground.

For a split second, my brain believed I was falling fast. But as I blinked and my perspective shifted, I realized I was descending, just not in a free fall. *Perhaps another invisible platform?* Not wholly comfortable with the sensation but stable enough to get my bearings, I tried to figure out exactly what I was traveling through. The best I could muster was that the surrounding walls were actually dirt, stabilized with something. I squinted. *The fungus?* The shaft I was moving through wasn't very wide, not even wide enough for me to spread my arms out, so I leaned a little closer to get a better look. *Yup.* I was fairly confident the dark swirls and lines were the same stuff that was on the Holy One and the spire. The only difference was that, as I descended, the fungal substance glowed.

The effect was beautiful in a terrifying sort of way. I wasn't sure how long I moved downward, but several of the patterns I saw repeated themselves. All those years of following my father, listening to his lectures, and watching him work kicked into gear.

Sam, are you there?

I heard a bit of static, but the ship responded. [SIGNAL IS AT FIFTY PERCENT AND DECLINING.]

Can you record what I'm seeing?

[IMAGES WILL BE LOW RESOLUTION. SIGNAL AT FORTY-THREE PERCENT.]

Just get what you can.

[RECORDING. SIGNAL AT THIRTY-FIVE PERCENT.]

I slowly turned, taking in as much of the patterns and shapes as I could.

[SIGNAL AT ELEVEN—]

I was unhappy on a few fronts. First, I was bummed I wasn't able to record more before the signal cut out, and if I got into a terrible situation down there, I had no backup. I shrugged. *Who am I kidding? Even with Sam, what would I do?*

Eventually, the platform stopped. That was the first time in my life that complete silence surrounded me. I could hear no background noise of engines running or various tech, just pure silence. The effect created the sensation that an invisible weight had lifted from my shoulders, and I was immensely lighter in body and spirit.

Once I stepped off the platform, the surrounding space grew, and the darkness stretched off in both directions. *Great, which way do I choose?* The fungus, or whatever it truly was, illuminated both choices. To the left, the light appeared to be reflecting off something metallic. I took a step in that direction, and the light faded.

Wrong choice, then? I turned to the right, and the light resumed, pulsing in gentle waves as it guided me. *Gotcha.*

I wouldn't recommend making that a goal in life: moving through dark spaces, following some weird, glowing fungus. But I was feeling like that was my new normal.

The tunnel wasn't long, and it opened up into an enormous cavern. I had no clue about the actual dimensions, only that the *Samaritan* could land there and still leave plenty of room left over for a party. The glowing fungus spread throughout the cavern's earthen walls, the twinkling light spiraling upward until it disappeared into the illusion of stars above me. I took a step closer to admire the intricate shapes the fungus had grown into. It seemed to congregate around bits and pieces of stone embedded in the earth. And upon closer inspection—I maintained a healthy distance—the fungus appeared to have forced itself into the minute fissures in the rocks.

When I turned to get a better look at the interior of the cavern, my heart about failed. In the center of the room stood three Darquets on some type of raised platform made entirely out of fungus. Their bodies faced inward, their backs arched and arms thrown up to the fungal sky. At first, I thought they were statues, but as I waited and watched, I noted their chests slowly rising and falling.

"Hello?" I whispered.

Even a noise that soft felt wrong in that place. But when they didn't answer, I took a few steps forward to inspect the Darquets. They were all female, and the fungus covered their bodies in the same strange patterns I'd noted on the earthen walls. The pulsing lights moved from the walls and across the floor—earning a startled squeak from me as it ran under my feet—and spiraled up the bodies of the three Darquets.

The light pulsed three times then, on the third pulse, pooled in their eyes. That was a little creepy. The Darquets turned and stared at me. *Yup, now it's a horror show. Great.*

I backed up, and the Darquet nearest me turned and stepped off the platform, fungus clinging to her like strands of silk.

"You shall be judged," she said in a voice as cold as ice. She raised a hand, and the fungus erupted from her fingertips like a spider shooting out its webbing. Before I could scream or run or faint, the fungus coated my body, winding its way up over my skin until it settled around my mouth. I bit down hard on the inside of my lips and tried to twist away, but the fungus shifted and moved up through my nostrils and down through my ears.

The heroine in a story would've let out a full-on bloodcurdling scream right then. But I couldn't.

15

Fungus Town

The fungus moved through my body. It slithered down the back of my throat, coating my tongue, and forced itself through my lips until it coated the outside of my mouth. Within seconds, the fear vanished, and the peace I'd felt during my blackouts reappeared. But instead of being wrapped in a warm cocoon of light, I was gently swathed in a cuddly nest of glowing fungus. Shifting patterns of pulsating light surrounded me. Repeated flashes of light danced off to my left then moved above me, below me, then to the right. Softly curling tendrils moved and rearranged into geometrical shapes, simple yet complex, over and over again.

I felt bliss. My thoughts drifted away, and I stopped trying to analyze and catalogue the experience and relaxed into the peace of it all. I knew without a doubt that whatever the fungus was, it held no ill will toward me. What was more, I could sense another presence—more than one. Hundreds or thousands of sentient minds surrounded me, pressing down around me with a sense of urgency.

And with one voice, they spoke. "Foundlings. Sanctuary. Reclamation."

I don't understand.

"Speak. Outside. Speak."

My mind was addled, fuzzy, and confused. *What does that mean?*

"Speak. Outside. Speak."

Speak... outside? I didn't know what outside was. For a moment, the concept was foreign. Then the pulsating light dimmed somewhat, and I heard the words again.

"Speak. Outside. Speak."

Outside. I knew that word. *Am I inside? If so, where is the door to outside?* As if waking from a dream, I knew I had arms and legs and tried to lift them. But if I was moving, I couldn't tell.

I don't think I can make it outside.

The fungus coating my tongue shifted and wormed its way down my throat. My lips were pried open then closed, and I realized what the consciousnesses wanted.

"You want me to speak out loud?"

I didn't receive a solid yes, but when the voices moved on, I assumed I'd guessed correctly.

"Division. Discord. Disillusionment."

"I'm not following," I said. Part of me didn't want to or just plain couldn't. I was too far gone in la-la land to make any sense of what was happening. But the voices persisted.

"Longing. Need. Unity."

Emotions not my own drifted past me—grief,

loneliness, desperation, resignation—and they cut through some of the peace, tiny shards of reality that brought glimpses of clarity.

"Are you..." I stopped. "Can you tell me what's happening to me?"

"Searching. Needing. Asking."

"Is there something you want from me?"

"Searching. Needing. Asking."

"I need to understand if I'm going to help you. What are you?"

I sensed frustration, overwhelming and suffocating.

"Triune. Triune. Triune."

Not helpful. But okay.

"A triune? Can you clarify?"

"Lost. Need. Triune."

"Okay. Something has been lost. You need help finding it?"

The voices receded into a faint, incomprehensible buzz, and I could feel the fungus shifting within me.

I'll spare you the description of what I experienced as it left my body.

But once it was gone, an unshakable feeling of loneliness settled around me, and I couldn't help but cry. For a moment, I'd been connected to an immense network of minds, a type of collective consciousness, and its departure was keenly felt.

"You have been judged. And deemed worthy."

I blinked away the tears that had formed and stared up at the pure-white eyes of the female who'd sprayed me with the fungus.

"That's... great?" I squeaked, feeling a little

light-headed. "Can you tell me what that means, exactly?"

"You've been cleansed of the artificial and replaced with The Third."

"Um… what?"

"Go and seek. Find and deliver. Mend and divide."

Right. I guess the Holy One wasn't kidding when she said the answers would come slowly. More like not at all.

I pictured Cain sitting in a chair, staring at the door, waiting for me to return. *Cain knew about the Holy One. Did he know about this? If he does, well… I'll have to cross that bridge when I come to it.* If not, I had a whale of a story to tell him.

The female blinked, and I noted the two who had remained on the platform shifted their gaze from me to her. Their arms moved in sync and reached out to her, but the female didn't move to rejoin them on the platform. Instead, she took a step toward me, and the two on the platform frowned. I wasn't getting good vibes from them.

"Turen?" the female asked.

"What about him?"

"Cain." The female frowned, her brow furrowed, and a hint of color appeared within her white eyes, a soft glow of amber.

The two females shifted their weight and leaned toward their companion. The fungus slithered across their bodies and snaked down their arms until thin tendrils rose from their fingers like snakes dancing to some distant melody.

"Cain is not his name," she said.

Not knowing where the interaction was going, I decided not to argue with the creepy fungus lady. "Right. It's a nickname. Turen ed-Suren is his given name."

"Yes. Turen ed-Suren. My name. His name. Elea el-Alea ed-Suren. My name. His name."

The hint of amber widened, and I caught sight of her pupils before the dancing fungus slithered across her back, over her shoulders, and up her neck. It twisted and turned, coating her face as her head tilted and they forced her back onto the platform.

Watching in shock and a fair amount of horror, I could think of only one explanation.

Cain's sister.

"Wait."

But a wall of the fungus exploded out of the ground, stopping me in my tracks. It shivered and shook, and I definitely got the message. When I took a step back, the fungal wall grew still. When I took another for good measure, it sank back into the ground.

"Can you at least talk to me?" I called out, standing on tiptoe to see above the divide.

I received no answer beyond a glance over her shoulder as the three stretched their arms skyward. The hint of amber faded until her eyes were completely white once more.

Great. How in the world am I going to—

A distinct crackling noise filled my head, accompanied by a high-pitched whine. I slapped my hands over my ears and winced.

[Ca... ease... or...]

Sam. I thought I'd completely lost the signal. I was

torn. Standing in front of me was Cain's sister, one of my objectives for coming to Dar. *But talk about your huge hiccups. How in the world am I going to help her?* I didn't have any tools at my disposal to do so in the moment, so I made my decision.

I turned and moved back toward the tunnel I'd descended through. If Sam or someone on the ship was trying to contact me, I needed to know what was going on. I stepped into the center of the tunnel, and after a brief moment of wondering if I needed to do something else, I gently ascended.

Sam? I'm here. What's up? Though I used no official language, the AI got the drift. She was catching on.

[AN *IG* VESSEL HAS ISSUED A... DESIST ORDER. COMMANDER LIO HAS ISSUED ORDERS TO ENGAGE THE OVERDRIVE... IS ATTEMPTING TO BYPASS THE CAPTAIN'S AUTHORITY... MMAND CODES.]

I wasn't surprised. Yilmaz had warned me. She and her cronies were bound to catch up to us eventually. And Lio was responsible for the ship and the crew. He might've sympathized with what I was trying to do, but he had a duty to perform.

Sam, follow his—

A second high-pitched squeal interrupted me, followed by a burst of static. "What in Jupiter?"

I doubled over in pain, the static buzzing in my head.

Leave. Now. Sanctuary.

Wincing, I straightened and looked around. I was still alone on the platform, but the fungus coating the walls was glowing with abandon. "I'm doing that.

Hold on," I muttered and reached up to touch my ears. My fingers came away warm and sticky.

Leave. Now. Sanctuary. The voices screamed.

The pain from the static and the voices all fighting for dominion in my head drove me to my knees. I gripped my head with my hands, unable to do anything but rock back and forth, praying the pain would go away.

If I could have clawed my way to the top, I would have, but I was forced to wait until the invisible lift made it back to the surface. Gritting my teeth, I looked up. I was almost to the top. When the platform stopped, I made myself move, and once clear, I collapsed onto the ground.

After a hiss and a pop, the static was accompanied by another fair bit of pain. I grimaced and touched my ears again, my fingers becoming coated in blood. A shadow loomed over me, and I looked up at the disapproving gaze of the Holy One.

"It would seem you've been judged... worthy." That word was completely laced with venom. If she'd been a Pli, I would have expected little poisoned darts to shoot out of her mouth as she spoke.

"Not exactly a walk in the park," I muttered. The pain was receding, and I pushed myself up and stumbled a bit, not very dignified. But I sidestepped around the Holy One and moved out from under the canopy of the spire. I needed to know what was happening on the *Samaritan*.

Sam? Report. Come in, Sam.

Sam, I need you to report. What's going on out there?

Squinting, I looked up at the crystal-blue sky then grimaced. *Fool, you can't see anything from here.*

"If you would listen, child, I will tell you," the Holy One snapped.

Oops. I hadn't realized she'd been trying to talk to me.

Satisfied that she had my attention, she said, "They have granted your ship sanctuary. It is under the protection of Dar now."

I gaped at her. "What?"

She grimaced and raised an arm, turning her hand back and forth as she studied the webbed fungus that had returned to her skin. "It was decided."

Sanctuary—that's what they... it said down there. "The fungus? It's giving the *Samaritan* sanctuary?"

The Holy One nodded. "Yes. But it isn't a fungus. It is the Third. Respect is owed for what it has done."

"Believe me, I'm grateful. More than grateful the... Third is helping us out," I said.

"No, child. That is not what I mean. You have been judged and deemed worthy. You and the male shall live. It would appear you've been granted a gift none outside of Dar have received in eons. You've been cleansed of the artificial and replaced with the Third."

And suddenly, my plate was full. "Right. You explain what that means while we head back to where we left Cain. Then I need to get in contact with my ship," I said as I crossed to where the platform had been. I didn't know if it was still there or how everything was supposed to work, but I planned to move forward like I knew what I was doing, and everyone else would follow. *Right?*

As the Holy One stepped beside me and we started our ascent back to the cities in the sky, I turned and stared at her. "Oh, and one more thing. Why is Cain's sister down in fungus town?"

16

Revelations

"You are bleeding," the Holy One said in response to my question.

"How astute of you," I mumbled, annoyed she'd sidestepped my question. "But what about Cain's sister?"

"It is not of my—" The Holy One's entire body froze.

I stepped back, uncertain of what was about to happen, and watched as the Third moved to cover her face.

She blinked once, then her head tilted to the side. "They have granted you a gift. You have the capacity within you to heal from such wounds."

Her voice didn't sound any different, but even with the hard-to-read, creepy white eyes, I sensed another presence staring at me from within the Holy One. And the words certainly weren't what I'd expected to hear.

"Right. And I can fly too. Now, what about Cain's sister?"

She pursed her lips, and the Third shifted along her neck. "You speak of an individual. Were you not greeted by the embrace of the Third?"

"If you mean wrapped up in the fungus, then yes,

I've had the pleasure. But I want to know why Cain is sitting in a room somewhere believing his sister was arrested and thrown in Darquet jail for trying to get their family's heart stone when she's actually down in a hole?" I paused. "Or is that what you consider jail?"

The Holy One's fingers twitched, and the Third shifted across her skin again. "A revelation which should not have happened."

"Fine. But it did. Why is she down there?"

"If you are referring to what you witnessed within the Third's embrace, you must take time to see the blessing which was bestowed upon one such as her."

"Blessing? Being stuck down in a hole? With some kind of hive mind fungus—" I held up a hand. "No, my mistake. With the Third crawling all around inside of her?"

"It is of the highest honor, to be chosen as a vessel."

I narrowed my eyes. "Is that you talking or the Third?"

The Holy One's mouth opened, and I heard the words but didn't see her lips move at all. "Honor. Demands. Salvation."

Were those words supposed to be spoken in that order? If we were moving away from random cryptic words to something a bit more cohesive, I wasn't sure I liked the implications. "Salvation? So being chosen as a vessel is saving Elea in some way?"

"Salvation. Forced. Servitude."

"Where I come from, those ideas faded away a long time ago," I said. "But if you're trying to tell me something more, I'm not tracking."

The Third moved back and forth across the Holy One's mouth and eyes, and her fingers curled into fists. I shifted my weight, working to balance myself and preparing for anything to happen.

Her mouth snapped shut, and her eyelids blinked in rapid succession, until the Third left her face and stopped to rest in a tangled mess on her neck.

"You okay?" I hesitated to ask.

The Holy One pursed her lips but nodded. "It is of the highest honor to be chosen as a vessel."

I opened my mouth to tell her she'd already told me that but changed my mind. I couldn't be sure, but I had a sense she might not have been in complete control of herself.

I asked a different question. "If it's such an honor, then why aren't you down there? How come you get to go wherever you want?"

The Holy One pulled her shoulders back. "Many may be considered conduits for the Third, but only a few are chosen to become one. None expected they could choose an impure child of Dar for the honor. But she was tried, as all who take the path she treads, and the Third revealed her authentic place within its embrace."

So much in that little exchange needed to be unpacked. The Holy One wasn't telling me the complete story, that was for sure. But I put those comments in stasis for the time being.

"The *Samaritan*, then?"

"Heal your wounds."

I huffed. "Most everything comes with an instruction

manual. I seem to have misplaced mine. Care to fill me in?"

"Ask, and it shall be given."

That sounded familiar. "Heal me, oh great fungus."

"Is this how you would treat another's sacred ways?" she snapped.

The Holy One had a point. I was being rather flippant about the whole deal. I did think they should grant me a bit of leeway, considering my level of frustration, but theirs was a completely different culture, with ideas and beliefs I didn't understand. *Who am I to belittle what the Holy One is telling me?*

Cool it, girl. "I beg your forgiveness," I said with sincerity. "I was out of line. But I need a bit more clarification."

"Our cosmos is vast, driven by forces unseen and unknown. Who are we to establish the limits to its great wonders? Dar was once shrouded under a cloak of misconceptions, and there are some who still cling to the ancient beliefs. But the presence of the Third has opened the eyes of Dar, and we embrace the wonders which await, and we guard what must be kept hidden from those who might seek to abuse such things."

I let out a deep breath and worked to calm my anxious thoughts. I was trapped on a tiny little platform, way up in the clouds, with nowhere to go. Working myself up wasn't going to do me any good, and we still had quite a way to travel before we were anywhere near where we'd left Cain. I needed to treat this like a help desk call. I considered how I would've worked through the problem.

"The Third. Can we start there? How would you describe it?"

My questions earned a grudging nod. "That which must be kept hidden, protected from all who would abuse its power."

"Biologically, can you expand on the Third in those types of terms?"

"It is the Third." She lifted an arm, and the Third wiggled and rearranged itself in a new pattern. "The Third exists of its own, yet it is still only a part of a larger whole."

Engines ignited. *A part of a larger whole. Mend and divide. Were the words adequate, or was I working with a poor linguistic translation? Mend the divide? Help what was lost?* Those emotions and ideas were similar to what I'd felt when lost in the light. And Cain had said my blackouts resembled the trances of the Holy Ones. The blackouts had started after I'd been injected with the smart-bots and seen the bright flash of light from the Star Eaters on Lunar 5.

Overdrive engaged. *Holy crusty crab pinchers of Jupiter.* "You said what was artificial has been replaced by the Third?"

The Holy One nodded.

"You're telling me the smart-bots have been removed? And in their place, I've got the Third inside of me?"

"Ask, and it shall be given."

If I could have sat down, I would've. *Talk about a lot of information to absorb all at once.* I felt light-headed at the revelations. "How? How do I ask?"

"Speak with the Third."

I looked down at my hands, inspecting them for any

hint of the Third. But the Holy One reached out and took my hands in hers.

"The Third chooses the Holy Ones and manifests itself in different aspects. You shall not find what must remain hidden from those who would abuse it." She released my hands. "Ask."

Here goes nothing. "I… I humbly request you… I mean, the Third, if you would be so kind as to repair my ears? My eardrums? I guess whatever cut off my connection with the *Samaritan*?"

The Holy One bowed in supplication. "A most generous offering."

I stood there, frozen, unsure what would happen. At first, nothing appeared to change, but I gradually felt pressure building in my ears until my head felt as if it was about to pop.

For a moment, I was afraid I'd blacked out again. But the flash of darkness was gone in a second, and so was the pressure. Gingerly, I touched my ears, and my fingers came away clean.

Sam?

[PLEASE, HOLD.]

Good grief.

Sam, what's going on? Report.

[WE HAVE BEEN OFFERED PROTECTION. COMMANDER LIO HAS ACCEPTED PER MILES'S INSTRUCTIONS. WE WILL MAINTAIN A SYNCHRONOUS ORBIT.]

What happened? Did the IGJ fire upon the ship? Is that why comms cut out?

[NEGATIVE. THERE WAS A DISRUPTION WITHIN MY NEURAL MATRIX. IT IS CURRENTLY BEING REPAIRED.]

That didn't bode well. That type of breakdown had all but vanished a few decades before.

Any diagnostic results on the disruption?

[NEGATIVE. DIAGNOSTIC PROGRAMMING IS STILL RUNNING. ESTIMATED COMPLETION TIME IS IN THREE HOURS.]

Long wait. Let me know when the results ping.

[AFFIRMATIVE.]

"What else can the Third do?" I asked the Holy One.

"Whatever it wishes to grant. Healing. Communication. Glimpses of the past. Foretelling of the future. For each Holy One, the experiences are unique. We do not seek but are vessels to receive."

The Third had picked the wrong vessel, if it thought I was going to sit around and wait for it to bless me with whatever it provided.

Sam. New order. I want Miles brought to where Cain and I are assigned.

[ORDER RECEIVED. A SHUTTLE WILL BE PREPPED AND LAUNCHED WITHIN THE NEXT HALF HOUR.]

And Sam? If the bugger tries to resist, bring him to me in restraints.

[UNDERSTOOD.]

"Holy One, we're going to have another guest joining Cain and me. I want him brought to me as soon as possible."

"Clearance must be received—"

"I mean no disrespect—I really don't—but the Third has chosen me, making me akin to a Holy One?"

She nodded.

"Great. Then I gather that affords me a wide berth of command."

She hesitated.

"You said you weren't ignorant of what's going on out there. Well, whatever it is, is connected to what's going on with me. And there's a certain piece of space trash who holds more information than he's let on. It's time he spilled the beans."

I saw a hint of irritation in the way she pursed her lips, and when she didn't respond, I took a closer look. Those pauses of silence weren't just her thinking about a response—she was communicating with someone else or a multitude of someone elses. Either way, I didn't care.

"You tell whoever is listening that I'm not asking this time. I'm telling you. All of you. You allowed me on Dar, you took me to be judged, and I passed. With flying colors, if I do say so myself. So you're going to let him through and bring him to Cain and me. Understand?"

The Holy One sighed. "It will be granted. But you have been warned. Any disturbances to the children of Dar will not be tolerated."

17

Tangled Webs

"Are you okay?" Cain asked as I closed the door behind me.

Where to begin?

"Sit down. We need to talk." *What's the best way to break the bad news, give it first or save it until last? Or how about just sidestepping the whole issue and pretending it doesn't exist?*

He narrowed his eyes but didn't protest as he bent back down to sit. We'd talked about trust and formed a tentative bridge between us. Before us was a colossal test of that trust.

<*Trust me,*> I whispered to him.

He gave me a curt nod, and I took up my battle stance, pacing back and forth in front of him.

"First things first. And I really need you to stay as calm as possible. Please. We've got a lot to work through."

He nodded, but I noted his fingers digging into the bedspread. Maybe pacing wasn't the best way to deliver the news. I went and sat down next to him. I bit my lip and looked down at my feet then up at his worried expression. My fingers slid toward his, and I wrapped my hand around his.

"You told me they imprisoned your sister for trying to steal your family's heart stone, right?"

Cain nodded, and he tightened his grip. "That was the report my mother received."

"Okay. No other news? Or hint as to what might happen to her? Nothing in Dar lore your mother might have mentioned?"

Cain narrowed his eyes. "No. Why?"

"What's your sister's name?"

I wasn't sure how else to approach the truth and was ready to just rip the bandage off. *Just do it and get it over with.*

He narrowed his eyes but answered, "Elea."

"Okay." *Here we go... Three... two... one... rip.* "I met your sister."

Cain stared at me then shot off the bed and whipped around to look at me. "In the Halls? An Ascended? That's impossible. She was tried as a criminal. They wouldn't accept someone like that. Besides, she's not full-blooded Darquet." Then he took up pacing.

"This is remaining calm?" I asked but quickly sobered. "It's complicated... I think. I was taken to the Spire of the Third? Ring any bells?"

"No," Cain growled.

"The Holy One told me I would be judged and, if I passed, implied the two of us would be safe."

"What does that have to do with—"

I raised a hand. "I'm getting there. I traveled down into a cavern, deep within Dar. That's where I saw your sister. She's not a Holy One. I think she's actually something more than that, if I'm putting the information together correctly."

The look of pure anguish on his face wounded me. I really should've thought my delivery through a bit more. But I had a lot to catch him up on before Miles arrived. I wanted Cain and me on the same page when I confronted the annoying man.

He staggered back. "What? How is that possible?"

"I don't know. And I swear we'll get her out. I think… I think she asked for help? I'm not sure. Still getting the hang of all this, but for now, she's okay. Or at least, I'm pretty certain she is."

Cain clenched his jaw. "Take me to her. Now."

I stood and walked over to stand in front of him, forcing him to stop. "I would if I could. But right now, we've got other issues we need to discuss. I know none of this is what you want to hear, but I'm calling in every ounce of trust you can muster. Can you do that?" *<Please? We'll rescue her, I promise.>*

Cain stared at me then, in an unexpected gesture, pulled me close. "I trust you," he whispered.

I grabbed his hand and led him back to the bed. I didn't care what kind of drugs Dr. Kell had pumped into his system to get him fit to come to Dar—Cain needed to be careful.

"First, I'll say it again. I really think your sister is okay for the time being, and believe me, I've got a slew of questions for the Holy One on that matter. And if we don't get any satisfactory answers, we'll ask the next person and the next and the next until we do. Okay?"

An odd mixture of emerald and amber appeared in his eyes, but Cain nodded.

I told Cain everything.

By the time I finished, Cain was up and pacing again. I wanted to tell him to stop, as the hitch in his gait was worsening with every pass. But he'd remained remarkably restrained as I'd filled him in about Miles and the IGJ.

So much for being careful. But perhaps working off his aggression before Miles arrived wasn't such a bad thing.

"And you think Miles knows about this… Third?" Cain asked.

"I'm betting so. Or at least an inkling. He's been pulling our strings ever since Epsilon's Station, like little puppets. But before he gets here, I need to know. What's your history with Miles?"

Cain stopped and stared at me, and I could read the hesitation written on his face.

"You're trusting me, remember?" I said as I moved back to stand beside him. I reached out to grab his hand. "This is important. We don't need any more surprises right now. Especially not here. I may hold some sway"—I brought a hand to rest on my chest, knowing what lay inside me—"and may have been a tad bit rude to the Holy One. Not my finest hour. So we need to be careful."

The term *rude* was a tad bit benign. I'd been insulting, and I knew it. But I rationalized my behavior away because of the shock of seeing Cain's sister and the arrival of the IGJ.

But before Cain answered, the doors to the room burst open, and the man of the hour arrived, accompanied by guards. Not one or two, but four very large male Darquets escorted Miles into the room. My smile might've been a little bigger than it should've been. An altercation must've happened, as Miles was sporting blood at the corner of his mouth.

I sighed. I wouldn't have minded being the one to punch him. But the day was young.

"Leave us," I ordered. That was a bluff—I didn't know if they would follow my orders or not, but after what had happened, with me passing my judgment, it was worth trying. The four guards bowed in supplication and backed out of the room, shutting the doors. Miles threw me a suspicious look before moving to sit in one of the chairs.

I blocked him. "Nope. You can stay right where you are."

I only meant to throw my weight around to get Miles to understand I was in charge and I meant business. He needed to drop the act, cut me some slack, and fill in the gaps. I wasn't expecting the Third to back me up.

When he smirked and tried to step around me, I bent over and coughed then gagged at a lump that formed in my throat. Cain stood next to me and rested one hand on my back while the other held my arm as my coughing grew exponentially.

Long, thin tendrils of the Third unfolded from my mouth and stretched and grew as they snaked over to a very shocked and probably disgusted Miles. In my hacking, I saw it wrap around his ankles before he had the chance to jump out of the way. Part of the Third anchored itself to the ground, while the rest wound its way up his legs and forced him to his knees.

After one last fit, I spewed the last of the Third from my mouth, but as I straightened, it reached back toward me. Instinct should have made me recoil, but I was so far past anything natural happening to me that I reached out to it. Fascinated instead, I let the Third move across the backs of my hands and wrap itself around my lower arms. The ends coiled into intricate patterns.

"Who's the puppet now?" I laughed and looked over at an ashen-faced Cain. "Too soon?"

Honestly, if not for all my weird and wacky experiences as a kid, I probably would have fainted. But having a xenologist as a father meant I'd seen my fair share of the weird and unexpected. And after everything from the *Rapscallion* to the *Justus* and now Dar, this was just another day at the office.

"The Third?" Cain asked. To his credit, he didn't move away but helped me straighten up. "This is what's inside Dar? My sister?"

"Your sister?" Miles butted in. "You found her?"

"That's none of your business," I said.

"Mahia."

I looked over at Cain. "What?"

He rarely spoke my name. That wasn't a good sign, at least not when we were with someone else.

"You asked about my history with Miles. It's not just my history but that of my sister as well. They were—"

"Elea and I were engaged once upon a time," Miles said for Cain.

I gaped at both men. "You've got to be kidding."

They both shook their heads.

"Well, that's a twist I didn't see coming," I muttered.

"But it explains some things." I stared at Miles and wondered who would want him as a brother-in-law. I couldn't even begin to image the family get-togethers. *No thanks.*

"How did someone like you end up being engaged to Cain's sister?"

"Underhanded trickery," Cain muttered.

"I would expect nothing less from a person like him," I said.

Miles shrugged. "It's the way of the worlds." He looked down at the Third wrapped around him. "Any chance this stuff isn't catching?"

"I don't know. Why don't you tell me?"

Miles frowned, and I leaned closer, pleased to note the Third tightening its grip on him. "Tell me this, then. How were you planning on getting me to Dar if we hadn't needed to come here because of Cain?"

A mad glint appeared in his eyes. "How do you figure that?"

I smiled. "You've known all along, haven't you?" I wriggled my fingers to jostle the Third. "Why else play me for a fool with the smart-bots and the Star Eaters? Was the tech a prereq for the Third? To let a non-Darquet bond with it?"

"You've lost me." Miles shook his head.

I leaned back. "I doubt that very much."

A serious look of concern washed over his face. "You're correct in assuming I would've found an angle to travel to Dar. Dr. Ashter and even your father… The work they did, a lot of it, points to the questions they had about this planet. But I didn't know what it might lead to, only that this was a place on my checklist." He shrugged. "But good old Cain here helped push it further up the list."

"If we get out of this," I said, "you're going to show me that checklist."

"Over a five-course meal… I'll consider it," Miles quipped.

Cain growled. "You'll do more than that."

<Don't throttle him just yet.> "Miles, I need to know. What options were the Star Eaters supposed to give me?"

For a moment, I thought he was going to give me one of his roundabout answers, but the teasing glint in his eye disappeared, and he looked down to study the Third. "They didn't specify. I made the arrangements with them because they promised if I could set up a face-to-face with you, then they would send another pair to meet with me, something I've been trying to do for ages."

"That's all I was worth to you? A potential meetup?" I gaped. I'd expected some big, glorious life-or-death scenario.

"Is that all?" Miles mocked. "You're kidding, right? I've been trying to catch a Star Eater for years. But they're slippery little buggers. And here you come, prancing onto the stage, and they're fawning all over you."

I laughed. The poor would-be emperor was jealous. "I think they've got good taste, then."

"Ouch. That's a rather low blow." Miles winced. He turned his attention back to the Third once more. "Look, all diabolical plans aside, I really am concerned about my well-being here. These kinds of entrapment scenarios don't end well. Ever take a jaunt down memory lane and watch some Old Earth horror shows? Especially that old genre, science fiction? They had some wacky ideas of what was out there, awaiting humanity if they ever made it to the stars. Can't say there probably aren't more than a few writers who are laughing in their graves and thinking 'I told you so' right about now."

"You're in an awfully chipper mood, for someone in your position," Cain growled.

I agreed. "Answer some questions, and we may decide to let you go."

"We?"

I didn't respond but continued to stare at him.

"Come on, Cain. Tell your girlfriend to let me go. For old times' sake, huh?"

Cain stalked forward, and his hand shot out, his fingers wrapped around Miles's neck. "Old times' sake? If that were the case, brother"—absolutely no affection at all appeared in that word—"then I would be well within my rights to kill you."

"Then do it, and get this over with. We've each tried our fair share of times to end the other. Declare victory. Go on."

"Cain," I snapped.

Seeing him without his tail was hard. I imagined it would have snapped back and forth a few times right about then. I felt the Third shift on my skin, and I spied a few of the threads between myself and Miles shake and produce tiny offshoots.

"Cain, we've got to play nice," I said. "For now."

Thankfully, he didn't question me, and Cain moved off until he bumped against the edge of the bed.

"Spill it, Miles. All of it," I ordered. "I suspect if you don't, the Third will have something to say instead."

Miles eyed me then let his body go slack. "Can't a guy have any secrets? I mean, where's the mystery? The fun?"

"Miles…"

"Fine," he grumbled. "But don't expect much, you hear?"

I huffed.

"What do you want to know?" he almost whined.

I decided to approach it from a different angle and try to catch him off guard a bit. "How are you connected with ChowHo Insurance?"

"ChowHo? Out of all the questions you could ask, you start with that one?"

I nodded. "I said I need to know everything. Spill it."

"ChowHo has corporate offices on Old Earth. A distant cousin or something like that started it. The monarchy runs a lot of money through them, if you get my drift."

Wanting to keep him off balance, I switched gears and asked, "Are you working with Lucas? Or with Mrs. Gol?"

"What?" Miles snapped, letting his mask slip again.

I didn't believe that was a calculated maneuver. My hunch was that Miles was growing accustomed to me and was getting sloppy, which suited me just fine.

"You dare to ask me such an… insulting question?"

"Of course," I smiled sweetly, "because here's what I know. ChowHo employed my father, Mrs. Gol was on the board of directors, and it's a business which could have its sticky little fingers in everything. Makes for excellent cover."

Miles shook his head. "ChowHo is many things, but cover for the lunatics running around blowing everything up? I don't buy it."

"Where did you learn about ChowHo?" Cain asked.

I looked at him and realized I hadn't included my sessions with Dr. Ashter on the *Samaritan* in my debriefing. "From a reliable source."

"Dr. Ashter?" Miles interjected.

"Maybe."

"Come on, honey, two-way street. You want information, you're going to have to give some too."

"You will remain civil," Cain growled as he stepped forward.

Miles sniffed. "Don't worry—I'm not stepping in on your territory. But fine. I'll try." And he threw me a wink for good measure.

I rolled my eyes. "Back on topic, boys. You're the one who's paying Dr. Ashter to work for you."

"For convenience. He might be a right bastard, but he is the foremost expert on the Star Eaters. Besides, don't you know about the history he had with your father?" Miles shook his head. "You give me whiplash. One moment, I think you're clever, and the next you do something so foolish."

I bristled at the insult. I'd let the conversation veer off course, and I had a sneaking suspicion a little thundercloud was brewing off to my left.

<*I'll fill you in later. Calm down.*> I didn't think that

helped and still sensed a strong chance of thunder later on.

"Well, I can assure you Dr. Ashter was nothing but civil with me and a bit more helpful than your crusty shell was being. So, you're saying ChowHo isn't a front for these sun-tattoo lunatics? Whoever my father was wrapped up with?"

Miles shrugged. "I'd bet my best set of VCR tapes on it. If they were, I would have known."

Got you now. "How?"

He realized his little slip of the tongue and grimaced. "You've never asked me if I sported any tattoos or not."

18

Families...
Can't Live with Them,
Can't Live without Them

Touché. I hadn't asked that question.

"And?" I asked, working hard to rein in my temper, not at Miles so much, but at myself. If the stinky waste heap had even a squiggle of a tattoo on him, I was going to break something. I was running around, knowing he had alternative motivations, but I'd never stopped to consider what that particular motivation was.

"See for yourself," he said.

"Stay there. I'll do the honors," Cain said before I could move. He almost lunged at Miles and pulled back the collar of his jumpsuit. Then, with a hearty slap on the man's back, he looked at me and shook his head. "It doesn't mean he wouldn't have it somewhere else."

"True," I agreed. "But my instincts tell me there is something important about the shoulder."

Miles smirked. "Now you're using that clever little

gray matter. Anyone could have it anywhere, but when it's in a certain place, with a certain type of ink, well, it helps weed out the wannabes."

I nodded and thought that over. It made sense. Lots of clubs and gangs used tattoos as an identifier, and those with higher security needs often embedded coding in the ink for verification. So I needed to add a scanner to my wish list. *Got it.*

"We know at least my father, Mrs. Gol, and Yilmaz have been or were a part of a selective breeding initiative, which is wrapped up with the smart-bots." I needed to ask one more question, though. It'd been patient, waiting its turn. "And the Holy One said that the Third replaced the smart-bots. So could the Third be what everyone is looking for? I have a hard time believing no one would've figured out the connections with the Darquets."

"Are you sure you're ready for those answers?" Miles countered.

"Yes."

"Good, then when you know, you can fill me in."

"Miles…" I growled.

"What do you think everyone's after? What's the age-old game always been played for?" he countered.

"Power. Control. Weapons in order to be the one in charge," Cain said as he walked up beside me. "That's an obvious answer. This time, you need to be more specific."

Despite all Cain's threats and posturing, I sensed his growing ire.

So did Miles, apparently. "Honest truth. I can't be

more specific than that. Look," he sighed, "you didn't find a tattoo because I had it removed right after... well, after everything happened with Elea."

"His sister?" I asked. "Miles, this back and forth, it's—"

"Let him speak," Cain growled.

<*Really?*>

"Really."

Okay, then.

"First, let me be clear. The monarchy isn't behind the tattoo group, only a part of it. When you're talking about selective breeding and all that, nobody does it better"—I wasn't sure I believed his point there—"than a monarchy. I wouldn't be surprised if, in the beginning, the monarchy played a more prominent role, but as all things taper and wane, the monarchy's attentions were drawn elsewhere by more pressing matters of maintaining control as more species struggled for dominance."

"How far back are you talking?" I had to ask.

Miles shrugged. "As far back as I know. The tattoo was more of a family rite of passage than anything else. There wasn't a grand sit-down explanation of what it stood for, only some trivial nonsense about unlocking the greatest mysteries the known worlds offered and how humanity was going to do it before anyone else.

"I never paid much attention to those things, to any of it. I was interested in diversifying Old Earth interests to keep up with the rapid turnover in the marketplace. With all the known worlds out there adding their genius to the pool, important ideas and technologies were cropping up every day. We needed to shore up alliances, build more trade relationships, if humanity was going to continue to be a player on the chessboard.

"So when an enterprising young Chancellor of the Aligned Worlds sent an inquiring message about a potential meeting, I jumped at the chance. We met off the books. I was just biding my time, building up a solid stock of relationships for when I would take the throne.

"Chancellor Heron often brought her children with her. Furthering their education, I believe she said." Miles threw Cain a caution look.

Cain scowled and crossed his arms. I understood how hard it was to listen to things that hit too close to the heart.

"As the chancellor grew in popularity, her schedule became difficult to navigate. A few times, I met with Elea instead of the chancellor. And from that, we grew... close."

I turned to Cain. "Really? You grew up with this guy?"

Miles laughed at that. "No. Cain was a wee little kid. Elea's much older. But I'll take it as a compliment you think Cain and I are around the same age. I'll pass it on to my cosmetics team."

"Of course you have one of those," I muttered.

"Purist ideology has been around since who knows when. Ugly ideas unfortunately tend to cling to the shadows. But the movement was gaining popularity. I didn't care, mind you, but my brother did. As did my aunties—pretty damned vocal about it all. But I'd hoped, as did Elea, that when I was emperor, our alliance could make a difference, change some opinions."

Miles stopped and looked at Cain then back at me. "Look, if I'm going to tell you the rest of it, then you must promise to keep this guy off of me. Deal?"

That didn't bode well.

"No deal," Cain snapped as I said, "Deal."

We looked at each other.

<Just for right now. We need this information. Afterward, you can do what you like.>

"Fine," Cain muttered.

Miles raised an eyebrow at our exchange but didn't press for any more assurances. I think he understood how easily he could take a lesson on flying—without a safety net.

"I loved…" He shrugged. "Elea was a good match. She was smart, well-read, and could put a Glipglow matriarch in her place like no one's business. All things considered, she would've been dynamite as empress, someone to whittle away the time with. But my aunties… Well, when they caught wind of my plans, they took matters into their own hands."

He stopped and glanced at Cain. "I swear I didn't know what they did until after."

"Miles…" I warned him.

His gaze never wavered from Cain. "My aunties caused a crisis within the Heron household which would divert the chancellor's and Elea's interests and time."

"Crisis?" I asked.

"My father," Cain said without emotion.

Uh-oh. *<Don't do anything rash. Please. Just hold on.>*

Cain hadn't moved, not even a twitch of an eye, which wasn't a good sign.

"My brother put me on lockdown, insisted I renounce my ties with the chancellor before I took the throne. But I refused. Spent a fair bit of time in a cold, dark place for minor rebellion. When I got out, thanks to a few loyal friends, I hightailed it off Old Earth and left behind any trace of my family that I could. That meant removing that stupid little sun icon from my delicate flesh.

"But that didn't mean I didn't keep up with the news or wasn't able to put two and two together, realizing they added up to five. So I began my collections and my own little hunting party into this great mystery humanity was supposed to unlock. If my family wanted it, then I was going to get it first. And I've been collecting bits and pieces ever since. Including you."

"Including me," I whispered.

During Miles's hour of confessions, the Third had unwound and pulled back, coating my arms. I'd been so wrapped up in what he'd been saying that I didn't notice until Miles got to his feet and stretched.

"Do you have your answers?" Cain calmly asked.

"For the most part," I replied offhandedly.

My attention was drawn to the varying swirls the Third was making, and I made a mental note to record them and see how they compared to what I'd seen in the tunnel. I couldn't be sure, but some of the designs I was seeing felt familiar. Either the Third was repeating patterns, which could indicate some kind of communication, or they were mimicking something I'd seen before.

"Cain, do you think—" I glanced up and realized I should have been paying attention to him.

He had Miles by the throat and was halfway to the door with him. <*Cain!*>

I rushed after them but couldn't do much. Miles wasn't putting up a fight, and even though Cain was still recovering, the rush of adrenaline pumping through him made him a force of nature.

He disliked Miles—no, probably more like hated Miles—because of the botched deal with his sister. I assumed a fair bit more lay on Elea's side of the equation than Miles was letting on, given Cain's vehement reactions to the man. But he'd just learned Miles's family was responsible for his father's death, so I could cut him some slack.

Cain shoved Miles through the doors, and we almost all went tumbling off the side of the walkway. Maybe some kind of latent instinctual Darquet trait in Cain told him where to stop. But if that was the case, it would've been handy if it'd shown up with my gene-mods. *But whatever.*

"You filthy piece of mucrac," Cain snarled. He took a small step forward, making Miles's heel slip on the edge of the invisible platform. "After all the time the two of you spent together, you knew how Elea would react, how close she was to our father."

I reached out and laid a hand on Cain's arm. "This won't solve anything."

"I don't care," he snapped. "If our father hadn't gotten sick and I had just kept my mouth shut, Elea wouldn't be here, trapped and used as a…" His voice broke, and tears glistened at the corners of his eyes.

A few shouts sounded behind us, and I glanced over my shoulder to see the guards hightailing it over to us.

"Cain, I get it. Believe me, I do. I spent years fantasizing about what I would do to everyone who'd laid a hand on my father, but this won't give you closure." I was likely going through some personal revelations of my own as I spoke. "The only thing that helps is finding the truth, making peace with it, and learning how to move forward."

Cain turned his head to stare at me, his eyes as black as night. "And how's that going for you?"

I cringed. <*Not well. But I'm trying. You can too. And you know what? If it doesn't work, then we'll figure it out. But we'll do it together, okay?*>

A familiar voice interrupted us. "Release him, or I will hold you for spilling blood on Dar."

The Holy One had been summoned or had been spying on us.

"Just give us a few seconds," I said. "Please. With my apologies."

<*Cain, as much as I hate to say this, we still need Miles. He's got connections where we don't. And I know he's still holding out on us.*>

"No doubt," Cain snarled. He shifted his weight, and Miles's eyes went white with fear. I think, up to that point, he hadn't believed Cain would follow through.

"I don't... want to die. Please, I—" Miles tried to croak.

Cain tightened his grip. "We can't all get what we want, now, can we?" he whispered.

19

A Whole Heap of Trouble

"You were warned," the Holy One said then snapped her fingers.

The guards rushed forward, grabbed Cain, then tried to drag him away from the edge of the platform as another guard snagged Miles. Together, they worked to try to make Cain release his death grip.

"Let him go!" I yelled and ran up to the guard who was manhandling Cain.

When the guard didn't respond, I punched him. That, in hindsight, was a pretty dumb move on my part. For starters, the punch hurt me far more than it did the guard. Second, it turned the guard's attention on me, which subsequently turned Cain's attention from Miles to defending me.

Cain lunged at the guard, and the unexpected maneuver threw him off balance. Together, they tumbled to the walkway. Cain wasn't about to let go, and neither was the guard. Each one tried to gain the upper hand, but all they did was roll around. At one point, they rolled right into me and knocked me down. I was perilously close to the edge. My left arm dangled out over the wide yonder of nothing.

<*Cain!*> I couldn't help but call out to him. I really thought I was about to briefly experience the joy of flight. My desperation gave Cain the surge of adrenaline he needed. As I watched from an upside-down perspective and, oddly enough, in slow motion, Cain slammed his knees against the guard's back then pushed at the guard with all his strength. He flipped the guard up over his head, and he tumbled into thin air.

Cain rolled over and grabbed my hand, pulling me back away from the edge. I twisted so I could watch in shock as the guard fell through the sky until he was nothing more than a speck against the clear blue backdrop. I thought they would have had a solution to someone falling off the edge.

Either way, we were in a heap of trouble. Not only had we put up a fight, but we'd spilled blood—not just any blood, but that of a pure-born Darquet. I'd read through the laws multiple times and knew whatever thin thread of respect I might have earned with the Third choosing me was lost.

The remaining guards hauled us to our feet, and the Holy One smiled viciously. The predator had finally ensnared her prey.

"You were warned about breaking our laws. Now that you have, *I* can deal with you as we should have from the beginning."

"What's that supposed to mean?" I asked and tried to twist away from the guard.

"Do you truly believe we would welcome you on Dar?

We've sacrificed everything in order to provide sanctuary, cutting ourselves off from the rest of the worlds and crippling our economy in the balance. The worlds may be scattered across the vast expanse of space, but surely even you should understand how interconnected the worlds have become."

"To provide sanctuary?" Cain snapped. "For who? Because when my family needed you the most, you turned us away, you sanctimonious piece of—"

"She's not talking about Darquets. She's talking about the Third," I interrupted. "And I think you've forgotten something."

I looked down at the Third coiled around my arms. *If ever there's a moment when you're going to help out, this would be it.* I paused then added, *Please.*

Nothing happened.

I glanced up at the Holy One, who continued to smile. "You may have been found worthy, but that doesn't mean you hold sway. We've given ourselves to the Third for generations. It needs us as much as we need it. Your feeble mind isn't going to persuade it otherwise."

"So you're controlling it? Or what, telling it what to do?"

"Consider it more of a negotiation. We provide refuge, and it shows its gratitude to the children of Dar in a most singular way." During a pause, the Holy One had to be communicating with someone else. Her smile fell away. "It would appear I'm being told we must hold you until we reach a consensus. No matter. The deliberations won't take long. There will be no choice." She glanced at the guards. "Put them inside and seal the building."

I didn't particularly care for her choice of words, and judging by the annoyed looks on Cain and Miles's faces, neither did they. The guards shuffled us back to the room we'd occupied and dumped us on the floor. Miles tried to rush one of them, but the guard was too quick and landed a fist in Miles's side. Miles stumbled back, spewing more than a few choice words, but the guards only snarled at him as they backed out of the room. The doors closed with a sickening thud, then a telltale zap informed us a force field had been activated.

"I hope they recognize the need for air recyclers," I grumbled.

Cain stood and moved over to the doors. Pounding on them, he yelled, "You've got no right to keep us here! We're not subject to your laws per the Diplomacy Statutes of the World Coalition. We claim our diplomatic rights under the authority of the Aligned Worlds."

"Come off it," Miles said. "They're not going to just let us walk out of here. We've seen too much. Besides, your diplomatic rights won't cover dear Ms. Orion."

Cain whirled and started to stalk over to confront Miles, but midway, he grabbed his side and fell to his knees. I rushed over to him, and before I could say anything, Cain looked up at Miles. "Mahia is my heart's blood. My immunity will cover her. It's you that doesn't have any protection. You renounced your rights to the throne, cut off ties with your family."

Miles grinned. "Not a hundred percent true. You know how things are, always a bit messy with the upper echelons of government and such. My brother may have kept my name on the books, just in case of…" He shrugged. "Well, who knows? But just in case."

"Both of you, knock it off. Your bickering isn't going to help us get out of this mess," I snapped.

They both grumbled but didn't put up much of a fight. I'm sure Cain had more than a few choice words he wished he could telepathically shout at me.

"We've got a couple of problems," I said.

"Really? Wow, you're so observant," Miles muttered.

I pointed at him and looked at the Third coating my arm. "Shut it."

Miles raised his hands and took a step back. "Loud and clear."

"Here's the deal. We need to snag a heart stone, figure out how to program it or whatever it needs, in order to get Cain back to a hundred percent, and rescue his sister. But that's not what's important."

"It isn't?" Cain asked.

"No. It isn't." I stepped back so that they could watch me, and I lifted my arms. As I did, the Third shifted again, into a different pattern. When I spread them apart, they changed once more. When I dropped them down to my sides, cascading lines of swirls decorated my skin. "The Third is."

"We'll find a way to… extract it," Miles said with a disgusted grimace. "It'll be easier to study it that way."

"No." I shook my head. "That's not what I mean. The Third. They somehow disabled and destroyed the smart-bots then took their place."

"I know you think that's the going theory, but it's not possible, darling. The smart-bots don't work that way. I know I lied about the whole message deal, but I know enough—"

"Miles, shut it and listen," I snapped. "The Third *are* the smart-bots. I've no doubt they're what the smart-bots were supposed to replicate. This is what everyone has been looking for, what they've been breeding toward for generations: humans who were genetically compatible with interacting with the Third. Why do you think Dar has developed a culture that is so fanatical about keeping track of its lineages?"

"Because they've been watching for Holy Ones. Or, rather, those that could interact with the Third," Cain said in a sour combination of awe and disgust.

"Exactly. Dar has quietly been doing what everyone else has been trying to figure out. Only they've done it under the radar. And not for the glory of having some kind of superpower, but because they've given the Third shelter, here on Dar."

"Alright, I'm following you. But why?"

I shook my head. "I'm not sure. The Holy One alluded to some kind of mutually beneficial arrangement." I turned to look at Cain. "Any thoughts?"

He shrugged. "I didn't grow up on Dar."

"Surely, you must have some kind of idea, though," Miles said. "Come on and think, man. Use that tiny little brain of yours."

Cain snarled but didn't respond.

"Both of you need to use your brains. Come on, guys, don't you get it?" I asked.

They stared at me for a moment before realization dawned on Miles's face. I decided to give Cain some leeway as Miles had been researching that stuff for years, so I would expect him to pick up on the bigger picture faster than Cain.

"The Third are connected to the Star Eaters," Miles said.

Cain had a look of disgust on his face. "Surely, you're not implying that Dar has anything to do with the cult?"

"No, he's not. We're talking about the real Star Eaters, whatever they may be. But we know one thing. The Holy One said that Dar provided sanctuary. Not for Darquets, but for the Third. So the question, then, has to be 'Is the Third hiding from the real Star Eaters?'"

That was a brilliant question. But it would have to be put on the back burner.

[CAPTAIN. WE'RE UNDER ATTACK.]

20

The Best Laid Plans...

Sam, repeat. Did you say you're under attack?

[AFFIRMATIVE. WE ARE UNDER ATTACK. THE DISRUPTION TO THE NEURAL MATRIX WAS A REMOTELY TRIGGERED MELTING CODE, HIDDEN IN THE DATA PACKET WITH THE SCRAMBLED TRACE-BACK CODING FROM THE OFFICES OF BLOODHEARST & STROBE. ALL POWER IS BEING SHUNTED TO CRITICAL SYSTEMS. COMMANDER LIO IS REQUESTING FULL CONTROL OF THE SAMARITAN.]

Cain must have noticed my slack jaw. "What's wrong?"

"The *Samaritan*. Hold on," I said.

Sam, are you sure it was from my lawyer's letter? The one you were working on unscrambling?

[AFFIRMATIVE.]

Putting two and two together wasn't challenging. Yilmaz had busted into my lawyer's offices and taken my father's letter. Adding a sneaky little trap would've been a piece of cake—carrot cake, mind you, because it's my least favorite. That was an underhanded thing to do—impressive, though, and something I should've seen coming. Also, that was a valuable piece of information I needed to tuck away because where one trap had been laid, more would be there. *Who knows what sticky little bumps in the road Yilmaz has laid out for me?*

"What's wrong with the *Samaritan*?" Miles asked.

"How do you know what's going on with the ship?" Cain asked on top of him.

I shushed them both. *Sam, I thought they'd granted us sanctuary*. But maybe our little escape with the guard had changed that agreement.

[NEGATIVE. THE IGJ HAS BREACHED DAR-CONTROLLED SPACE AND HAS OPENED FIRE. DAR IS RESPONDING.]

Holy crumb cakes. I hadn't expected the IGJ to go against Dar. But I should've realized how desperate everyone was becoming. Lucas showing up and abruptly destroying worlds had put a kink in the works. The commandant must've been feeling the pressure. Admittedly, I enjoyed the idea of Yilmaz sweating right then, but even as the pleasant image flashed through my mind, it sobered me up too. The woman was a dangerous adversary. If she'd ordered the attack on Dar, then she knew she had the power to win. Nobody makes that kind of gamble who thinks they're going to lose.

And the whole melting code suddenly made sense. Yilmaz was thinking ahead.

I'd maintained control of the *Samaritan* for long enough. Even if I'd been on the ship, I couldn't have helped. Sam had been my backup plan, but at least I had Cain and Miles with me. Three heads were better than one, and we would figure out what to do next.

Sam, I relinquish—

Wait. Not yet.

Scratch that. If I turn over full command to Lio, can I still maintain a link with you?

[AFFIRMATIVE. THIS LINK WILL REMAIN UNLESS THE CONNECTION ON THE BIOLOGICAL END IS PERMANENTLY DISABLED OR THE COMM TECH IS EXTRACTED.]

Great. Start recording.

I lifted my arms, slowing rotating them in my field of vision.

"Has she gone crazy?" Miles asked Cain.

"Not yet," I said. "Sam's recording the Third. I've got a hunch about something I need to know before I turn over command of the ship."

"Command?" Cain asked.

"Buddy, you missed a lot, didn't you?"

"No thanks to you," Cain hissed.

"Boys," I growled. But my irritation at the two of them was exactly what I needed. The Third shivered then changed shape. "Wait. Never mind. Keep going."

"Enjoying yourself?" Miles asked with a more than suggestive smirk.

"You know that's not what I meant," I said.

"You'd better keep a civil tongue about you," Cain growled. "Or else you might need some more time with your cosmetics team."

I don't know whether it was good or bad, but their banter lifted my spirits. And I noted the Third didn't move.

"Miles, I need you to rush at me. Try to hit me or something," I said.

Miles threw Cain an inquisitive look, but when he merely shrugged, Miles turned to me and grinned. "Whatever you want."

Then his grin slipped, and he lunged for me. For a split second, I thought I'd made a really dumb mistake. The look on his face was one of pure rage. I held my arms up to protect myself, and as I did, the Third twisted then shot out at him. They wrapped themselves around his forearms and yanked him off course. When he tumbled to the floor and started laughing, I let myself relax, and so did the Third.

The part of the strange creature that was still wrapped around my arms coiled into a myriad of different shapes. *Perfect. Sam, did you get all of that?*

[AFFIRMATIVE.]

Encrypt the files. Extrapolate the different shapes the Third may have been forming, then run them through your databases, along with what we recorded earlier. I need to know if they correlate with anything. I had one more thought. *And Sam, I know it's chaos up there, but if you can, show Dr. Ashter the shapes. Only the shapes, not the original source files. See if he recognizes any of them. Then let me know as soon as you get any hits.*

[ORDERS RECEIVED. COMMUNICATIONS MAY BE DELAYED DUE TO ENGAGEMENT.]

I understand. Thank you, Sam. One last thing. I'm turning over full command of the ship to Commander Lio.

Sam walked me through the steps to officially give up the role of captain, and when that was finished, I realized Miles and Cain had huddled together.

"Best buds now?" I asked.

"Just filling him in," Miles said as he leaned back. "Everything okey dokey?"

"'Okey dokey'? Where did you learn that?"

Miles shrugged. "Here and there."

I rolled my eyes. "Good grief." I glanced up at the roof, picturing what was taking place far above us. "No, everything isn't okey dokey. The IGJ have crossed into Dar territory and opened fire on the *Samaritan*."

"I've got to get back, then," Miles said as he hurried to the doors. He tried to pry them open a few times before he turned and sagged against them. "I've got sensitive information on that ship, and I won't let the IGJ get their grubby little hands on my toys."

"Really? That's all you care about? Your stuff? What about the crew you're employing? Care at all about their lives?" I snapped.

"Of course I do," Miles responded, affronted. "But they know what to do. That's why I'm paying them." He turned around and started feeling around the door frame.

Cain moved back to sit on the bed, holding his side.

I sat down next to him. "Bad?"

He shrugged. "The IGJ are nothing if not thorough in their work."

"I thought Dr. Kell had—"

"She did. As best she could. But there are more than a handful of ways to compromise an enemy."

I reached out and gently placed a hand on top of his. "I'm really sorry," I whispered. "If it wasn't for me, you never would have—"

Cain grabbed my hand and interlocked his fingers with mine. "It's me that should apologize to you. I shouldn't have let my guard down on Lunar 5. If I hadn't been weak and gotten captured, none of it would have happened."

I shook my head. "That's not true. We both know Yilmaz would have found a way. I suspect that woman gets what she wants."

"Not anymore," Cain said with a ferocity that made me shiver. "I won't make the same mistake twice."

I leaned against him and let my head fall against his shoulder.

"What do you think the Third is trying to tell you?" Cain asked.

"I'm not sure. And if it's trying to say more than these shapes it makes, I'm not hearing it."

"Perhaps it can communicate easier with a Darquet because of our telepathic abilities."

"A possibility. But I can communicate with you—" I stopped and flushed. "I mean... Sorry, I've somehow got the—"

"It's alright," he murmured. "You can say it."

I didn't want to. "Anyway. At least I'm not coughing it up anymore." That was an experience I didn't want to repeat.

"Look, are you two lovebirds going to help me, or what?" Miles called out.

"Only if you promise to behave," I responded.

Cain and I stood as Miles turned to face us.

"We need to get out of here in order to"—I raised my hand as Miles rolled his eyes—"rescue Cain's sister then find a heart stone. After which, we'll get you to the *Samaritan*."

"And us?" Cain asked.

I shrugged. "I'm not sure yet. Let's see where the Third leads us." I looked at my arms, and the Third rippled then settled into lazy circles and ovals. I hoped it would take us where we needed to go. *If not, well... I'll make it up as we go along. I mean, that pretty much sums up my life right about now anyway.*

21

Help Desk to the Rescue

"Alright, smarty pants, how do you propose we get out of here?" Miles asked as he threw himself into a chair.

"You know, with an attitude like yours, I'm surprised you've lasted as long as you have," I said.

To my pleasant surprise, Cain laughed. But I needed to stay focused and not let that delicious sound distract me.

"You heard the little pop, right? When they closed the doors?"

They both nodded. "Good. Then that means there's a force field surrounding either the building or the doors. We need to figure out which."

"And how do you think that's going to—" Miles started then stopped as I stared at him. "Nope. I will not be your little test subject."

"Fair is fair. Besides, Cain shouldn't, and I won't. I don't know what an electrical shock might do to the Third. So that leaves little old you." I smiled as sweetly as I could.

Miles didn't grumble too much more, at least not

audibly. He stood and marched over to the windows on the wall opposite the door. They weren't particularly large, just a hair wider than Cain was, which would be fortunate if my plan worked. Miles studied the windows for a moment then pressed a lever and shot me a triumphant look as the two panes slowly opened outward.

"Shouldn't have doubted you," he said as he went to duck through the windows.

"Wait, we don't know if it's—"

He pulled back and howled with laughter. "Did you really think I was that dumb?"

I glared as he picked up a chair and hurled it at the window. He wasn't quite as smart as he thought he was, for a rather loud pop sounded, and the chair bounced off the invisible field and almost smacked him in the face. He really should have stood off to one side and thrown the chair. But at least his actions made for a little levity.

"Not funny," he mumbled as I giggled and Cain smirked.

"At least we know."

"Dar law is strict, but the last I knew, the crime rate was minimal. With such severe punishments, there's little incentive for Darquets to break the laws. The IGJ are constantly modeling their updates on the worlds with the least bit of crime," Cain commented. "I wonder if they truly set this building up for containing individuals or if it was just something the Holy One had to work with."

"What are you getting at?" I asked.

Cain shrugged. "The IGJ have strict technical specs on how their detention cells are set up—nothing on the inside a detainee can access. It might sound simplistic to have to say it out loud, but most technology is built to cater to the shipping industry, with redundant backup systems and multiple ports of entry in case of emergencies."

I nodded. "Like on the *Whimsy* when I wanted to access the scanner from inside the room to add our biometrics."

"Exactly," Cain said with an appreciative nod.

"Exactly," I almost squealed. "Cain, you're a genius. Start looking for some kind of hidden control panel. There has to be one."

"Why?" Miles asked, but even though he questioned me, he started looking. "It sounded like we were establishing there wasn't going to be one."

"When I left, I asked the Holy One how they weathered severe storms. Guess what she said?"

"I'm waiting with bated breath," Miles muttered.

"Spoilsport," I huffed. "These buildings have shielding to protect them. And more than that, they can be detached from their moorings."

I moved to one wall and ran my hands along the smooth wooden surface. "If they built these buildings to protect, they're going to have some kind of control system inside. Whoever rides out the storm will need to reset the system or use comms or something, at least. If we find it, we can override the system and maybe even get this thing to detach."

"I think a floating building may garner some attention," Cain said as he grimaced and bent over to check the baseboards.

I shrugged. "We'll pass through that wormhole when

we get to it. For right now, it's what we've got to work with. If we can get to the ground, we'll at least be on even footing. We don't stand a chance up here with their invisible walkways. We would be too cautious, trying not to tumble to our death, to do much good."

"And what makes you think this thing will go down to the ground? I thought Darquets had some serious hang-ups about not hurting the ecosystem or some such," Miles asked.

"I don't. But the Holy One took me to the ground on some type of platform. I'm running on the assumption they built the buildings with the same tech, especially in the case of truly severe weather. With sufficient warning, the buildings could move closer to the surface, out of the path of severe weather."

"We all know what assuming makes us," Miles said. Then he crowed triumphantly. "Found it." He stepped back as a part of the wall popped open to reveal a brightly lit control panel.

"Perfect," I murmured and rushed over. The control appeared to be configured in a standard setup, but to my disappointment, the panel didn't sport the Confore logo.

"Well?" Miles impatiently asked.

"Give me a sec," I replied.

"Move. Give her space to think," Cain snarled.

In my periphery, I could tell Miles hadn't moved. Then Cain's legs came into view, and Miles's stumbled back. I couldn't play referee with them all the time. They were big boys and would have to figure things out on their own.

I tried hard to ignore their increasingly agitated

conversation, more like an argument, and to stay focused on the panel. Confore had developed a wide variety of control panels for a wide variety of products. I had to guess what the controls might do, and a chance existed that I would inadvertently set off an alarm or something along those lines.

The controls were labeled in Arnish, the dominant language on Dar. Through the course of reading through all of Dr. Ashter and Miles's files, I'd picked up a little of the language but not enough to fully translate.

"Either one of you speak Arnish?" I asked.

Hearing a muffled thud, I twisted around to see Cain shrug and shake his head.

"Really? You never studied it?" I asked Cain.

"Because of how Dar treated our family, my mother didn't allow us to study the language. When I joined the IGJ, there were universal translators at my disposal."

"A little lazy, perhaps?" Miles jabbed.

I raised an eyebrow at him. "And what about you, oh great would-be emperor?"

"Translators," he mumbled but then quickly brightened. "But I do have an excellent memory."

"Uh-huh, right. So you can read Arnish. Get over here."

They both came over and squatted next to me. I didn't miss the look of pain on Cain's face as he did so.

"How bad is it?" I asked softly.

He shrugged. "Nothing to worry about yet."

Translated from Mr. Tough It Out speak, that meant it was pretty serious but he didn't want me to be concerned about it.

"If the IGJ hadn't disabled my bioupgrades, I'd be able to translate this for you," he grumbled, a hint of self-loathing entwined in those words.

I reached out to grab his hand, but Cain jerked his away.

"Hey, I thought we were moving past this," I murmured.

Cain shook his head and snarled, "What good am I? Can't even help with something so basic."

He stood and tried to stalk off, but I hastened to stop him. I knew we were putting on a show for Miles, but I didn't care.

"Cain, we're going to get through this. And we'll fix what they took from you."

Isolating myself for several years meant I hadn't had tons of practice with relationships of any kind. I truly thought my words would have a soothing effect on him but evidently not. Cain staggered back as if I'd physically assaulted him.

"Fix me?" he hissed. His eyes darkened from violet to emerald, with a hint of something darker still. "Like I'm a broken piece of tech someone has called in and needs help to figure out?"

"Cain, I didn't mean—"

To my surprise and great annoyance, Miles stood and stepped in between us. "Calm down, buddy. She's only trying to save your scrawny—"

Cain roared and lunged for Miles, and to my astonishment, Miles just stood there—no defensive posture, no attempt to dodge. If I'd been him, I would have at least blinked. But he didn't. He stood there and didn't flinch as Cain's fist stopped a few millimeters away from his jaw.

"Is that what you need?" Miles asked. "A good old-fashioned beatdown? Don't like the suggestion there's something wrong with you?" He tilted his head to one side. "But hasn't there always been something wrong with you?"

Cain's eyes widened, and his hand dropped to his side. The darkness in his eyes disappeared, replaced by a very dull violet. He stared at Miles, glanced over at me, then looked back at Miles. Then, without a word, he turned his back on us and went to sit down on the bed.

"What in Jupiter's name was that for?" I just about yelled at Miles. "You've got a real bedside manner about you, know that?"

As I moved toward Cain, Miles reached out and grabbed my arm. "Let him be. Don't you realize he's putting on a brave face for us? The man's got issues he needs to confront if he's going to get through this."

"And what? You insult him to facilitate that healing?" I sneered. I tried to shake my arm free.

He only tightened his grip. "You've got no idea what he's been through."

I stared at him. "Really? Why don't you fill me in? Or is this going to be another one of your little guessing games?"

Miles shook his head. "If Cain can't get a grip now over something as trivial as that, what do you think it's going to do to him when he sees his sister? Providing we can get out of here at all?"

I glanced at Cain and realized I hadn't thought about

that. *How would it affect him?* He'd told me he felt responsible for her coming to Dar and getting trapped.

"It still doesn't make it right, what you said," I grumbled.

Miles released my arm. "Maybe not. But it's the best I could do. Cain needs to face his demons, just as you have. Because if he can't..." Miles shrugged.

He sat down next to me, his back against the wall, while I stared at the control panel. In a horrible, twisted way, Miles had a point. Cain hadn't ever come out and said it, but he'd hinted at the feeling all along, that there'd always been something wrong with him since he wasn't purely Darquet or purely human.

In my eyes, I saw absolutely nothing wrong with that. Beautiful things could come out of two entirely different species coming together. Unexpected blending and flourishes of the cultures, when grafted together, could create something utterly unique.

But if Cain hadn't grown up in an environment that celebrated those differences, then he wouldn't know how special he truly was. *When we make it out of here, I'm going to make sure he knows that.*

The key to that whole sentiment was whether we made it out—not just from the building, but Dar. And for that to happen, I had to focus, even if that meant pushing away the idea of running over to Cain, wrapping my arms around him, and letting him know he was perfectly fine just the way he was. *When did I get so sentimental?* I scoffed at myself. *Perhaps when Cain did the same for me. When he accepted me even though I thought I wasn't anything special after what Pops had done.*

Pops, my father—whatever I called him—was the man with a thousand different secrets and more than a few different faces, it turned out. And he'd had contact with the Holy One. That could lead me to believe he'd known about the Third, the real reason he'd wanted to come to Dar. *But what about Dr. Ashter?* I'd been surprised to realize that some didn't hold the man in high esteem. But after decades of breakthroughs and his constantly reminding people of his genius through his work, some people were bound to be jealous. *But Miles? Would someone like Miles be jealous of Dr. Ashter? Possibly. Miles really is more of an armchair xenologist than anything else right now, traveling about and collecting information about the Star Eaters.*

As my mind chewed on those thoughts, the distracted chatter did the trick subconsciously. I'd been fiddling with the control panel and not even realizing it. The panel popped off, revealing the intricate network of tech beneath it.

"Alright. Let's see what you remember," I said.

Miles leaned in next to me, and I waited as he mumbled and ran a hand over the writing on the back of the control panel.

"Try removing those two control chips." Miles pointed. The tech might not have been built by Confore, but because of the interconnectedness of the known worlds for a handful of centuries, all tech had similar engineering bases, enough that I felt comfortable doing what he said.

"See the base wiring?" he asked.

I nodded.

"Good, let's reconfigure it to these specs." He pointed at the panel, prompting me to turn and give him a blank look. Miles actually blushed. "Right. Here." And he walked me through the instructions though he stumbled over every third or fourth word.

We leaned back and listened for the telltale pop of the force field disengaging—nothing.

No worries. After a few rounds of discussion, we decided to put the base wiring back in place and reinsert the left control chip. Then I rewired it once again. That produced a nice, crisp pop, like that of a satisfying bubble blown from a piece of all-in-one-meal gum. Those are much better than any zip pocket.

"We did it," Miles commented with a silly grin. "I never doubted us."

"Uh-huh," I said. "Now, for the tricky part. How to detach the building and not send us flying off into the wild blue yonder." I knew we wouldn't have much time to experiment since I'd deactivated the force field.

Three sets of control chips were there, and we'd been working on the top set. As I studied the panel, the wiring configuration around that set felt familiar. When I looked at the other two, they felt foreign. *I can see why I felt comfortable messing around with the top one.* "You know, this looks like the setup for the DodgerCam Personal Ship master shielding controls, which would make sense. These buildings function like little personnel ships."

"And that revelation means what?" Miles asked.

"It means, if my crazy logic had any basis in reality, that the bottom set of control chips would have something to do with navigation," I replied.

I vaguely remembered the spec sheets for the DodgerCam. Confore had taken over designing and building the internal guts for the spacecraft the year after I started working for them. But they'd sold the specs—I can't remember to which company—not too soon after that.

The question was, even if I was right, what would disengage the mooring mechanisms?

"Here goes nothing," I mumbled. If what we'd done above disabled the shielding, then I would try the same to see if that disabled the moorings.

"Cross your fingers," I told Miles.

The man obliged and held up his hands with fingers crossed.

I took out the chip on the right side, redid the wiring beneath it, and held my breath. The effects were delayed and a tad bit of a letdown, if you ask me, but the building shuddered once, twice, then a third time. Miles and I got up and raced over to the window. We were moving.

"You did it!" Miles exclaimed and threw his arms around me in a big bear hug, shocking me. He pulled back and winked. "Don't worry. My eyes are on a different prize."

I gave him a little shove then looked out the window again. That was where my skills went out the window—no pun intended. "How fast do you think we're moving? And at what trajectory?"

Miles peered out and shook his head. "I don't know. Not my area."

"We're headed downward but picking up speed as we do," Cain stated behind us.

I turned and looked at him cautiously. After my earlier blunder, I wasn't sure what to say or what would be welcome. But he'd schooled his features into a neutral expression, and his eyes were a crisp violet.

"Worst-case scenario?" Miles asked, still watching out the window.

"We crash and die," Cain said bluntly.

I frowned. "Little harsh, but I don't think so."

Cain merely stared at me.

I sighed. "These things are supposed to protect the occupants in a severe storm, right? Why would they design them to just crash and kill everyone? I'm sure there's a safety net built into the tech."

"You mean the force field you disabled?" Miles asked.

Whoops. I rushed back over and quickly activated the force field. "Right. Now, we should be okay."

As the building trembled, I glanced over at Cain. He stood there, hands clasped behind his back, his face silhouetted by the window.

<*We'll be okay, right?*>

On the surface of the thought, I was referencing our immediate situation, but I knew I was really asking about something far more personal.

Cain half turned his head as though listening to me but not able to look directly at me. I thought we'd made progress after I woke up there in that room. But I was starting to question that. Maybe Cain had been putting on a brave face for my sake. With a sigh, I turned and leaned up against the wall, watching him. *When we get a heart stone, everything will return to normal. Cain will be fine.* But even as I tried to convince myself, I couldn't help but wonder if I was just telling myself a lie in order to feel better.

22

Thanks, Universe

I was adrift in a sea of warmth. If I'd felt peace before, it had been a poor comparison to the absolute bliss I was experiencing. A sea of endless light stretched out behind me, and in front were undulating beaches of darkness. I tilted my head back and, with a lazy smile, regarded the sky. A strange and beautiful mixture of reds and purples stretched across the dome as if the place was in a state of perpetual sunset.

The light gently pushed me closer to the darkness as the shimmering waves moved in and out from the beach. As I drew closer, I spied a plethora of twinkling blue lights hidden in the sand, strange pinpricks of light that wriggled and squirmed through the darkness.

An extremely annoyed voice yanked me out of my very pleasant and relaxing hallucination—two of them, actually. I blinked, and as my eyes opened, my mind snapped into focus, along with a sharp pain in my lower back.

"Mahia! Blast it, are you alright?" Cain was shouting while Miles grumbled about not being able to move.

I blinked again and noted a strange grid-like pattern of light and dark around me. As I took stock of my situation, I realized what I was seeing, and I couldn't help but laugh at the convenience of the situation.

"Either she's fine and is laughing at us, or she's finally lost it," Miles said.

The Third had protected us by creating a hard shell around me. As I looked through its webbing, I realized the Third must have a wicked sense of humor. Instead of creating individual cocoons for Miles and Cain, it had squished the two of them together. If I could have taken a picture, I definitely would have.

I tried to stand up, but the Third didn't move to accommodate that. *Are we not out of danger yet?* I stayed still and listened. I could hear the faint hum of the force field and also birdsong. The building wasn't shaking or trembling, and I didn't get any impression that we were moving at all.

Moving once more, I reached out and gently pushed on the Third. The rigid structure didn't have any give, and I wondered if it'd been damaged in the crash and used up all its energy or whatever fueled the strange creature in its effort to protect us. I didn't like that scenario.

The Holy One had said, "Ask, and it shall be given." Perhaps that's what I needed to do. I closed my eyes and concentrated on what I wanted, for the Third to unravel itself and come back to rest on my arms.

"We're safe now. You can relax."

At first, my words didn't appear to be working, but then I felt a faint tickle along my fingers, and the sensation spread across my arms. When I felt confident enough to open my eyes, the protective cages were gone, and the Third had wound itself around my arms.

"Thank you," I whispered.

"Get off me," Cain snapped as he shoved Miles.

"You're the one who had his arms wrapped around me," Miles said with a shiver of distaste.

"Quiet, both of you," I said, noting the hum I'd heard had grown louder. I stood and walked over to the window. "Fudgey scuttling crabs."

The hum hadn't been from the force field but the noise of a small battalion of Darquets headed right for us.

"I think it's safe to assume they've figured out their building moved," Miles muttered as he came to stand next to me. "What? Darquets can fly now?" He turned around and stared at Cain suspiciously. "You can fly?"

"No," Cain snapped.

"It would be safe to assume they have tech to let them move through the air. Not sure why they wouldn't wear that all the time," I mumbled, thinking of the guard who'd tumbled over the side of the platform. Of course, when one lived in a society that rarely experienced that type of violence, getting lax in following safety measures could become easy.

I dashed back to the control panel and turned off the force field. "We need to go."

"No kidding," Miles quipped. "But where to?"

"The one place I'm pretty sure they won't follow. And exactly where we need to go," I said.

"Pretty sure?" Miles asked. "I'd like a bit more of a guarantee than *pretty sure*."

"Then stay here," Cain said as he opened the doors and took stock of our position. "You mentioned the Spire of the Third?"

"Yes," I replied.

"I'd estimate we're roughly six kilometers out, which means we've got about thirty minutes of hard running." Cain twisted to stare up into the sky. "It'll be close, as long as they're traveling at top speed right now."

"We'll make it," I said. "We have to."

We really didn't have any other options. Either we survived, or it was game over. I had a sneaking suspicion the Holy One would override any other voices and make sure we received the highest level of punishment possible if she caught us, especially after crashing one of their buildings.

From what I could see, the structure itself hadn't taken much damage, but I noticed as I took a few steps away that a handful of trees had been flattened. The Darquets were fanatical about their ecosystem. *Whoops.*

"You'll make it," Miles said as he moved up beside me.

I gave him a quizzical look. That was perhaps the most serious tone of voice I'd heard from him yet.

He stared at me and smiled, a soft, genuine smile. "I know exactly what I am. Don't get any ideas. I'm not trying to be the hero. I've invested a lot of time and energy into you and working to figure out what has everyone so up in arms. I'll buy you time. Get to the Spire, save his sister, and figure out what in the hell is going on. Deal?"

The man was complicated, and I hated to admit how

much he'd grown on me. "How are you going to slow them down?"

He winked. "I've got a good memory, remember?"

"What?"

Then he leaned close and whispered. "Keep your eye on him and remember he had a rough childhood. Turen was only trying to figure out where he belonged. Try not to be too judgmental."

Before I could ask him any other questions, he raced back into the building and slammed the doors. With a loud pop, the house trembled.

I burst out laughing. "You've got to be kidding me."

Cain moved past me and didn't look back. "We've got to go."

I had to watch, just for a moment. The building lifted off the ground and slowly ascended. I didn't know what Miles was planning, but at least it would be some kind of distraction.

With one last chuckle at the absurdity of the situation, I turned and took off after Cain. By the time we were less than half a kilometer from the tower, my legs and lungs were burning.

Do you know what the biggest business venture is? Not tech or spacecraft or hab units. Fitness centers. When you flit about space and hop from planet to planet, each with their unique grav specs, maintaining optimum physical health is key. Even with the plethora of bioupgrades available, if you're not in relatively good shape, good luck.

Dar's grav was slightly higher than Old Earth's, which was what they based the grav of Original Luna on. I hadn't gotten in a good workout since leaving for the *Starshine*, and I was definitely feeling the lack of exercise.

I had to stop, and I bent over, hands on thighs as I sucked in painful gasps of air. Looking up, Cain stopped, and when he turned back to check on me, he wobbled to one side then collapsed to the ground.

You selfish fool, I screamed at myself as I raced over to Cain. I hadn't even taken a second to consider what running would do to him. If the IGJ hadn't muddled about with his body, he would've had bioupgrades to compensate for various gravs, but the upgrades had been removed or damaged, according to Dr. Kell.

"Cain." I shook his shoulders. "No, Cain. Dammit!" I shook him hard and yelled at him, but he'd passed out.

His skin was nearly white, and it was cold and clammy to the touch. <*Not again. I can't lose you again.*>

And I won't. If ever there's a time to help me, this is it.

I laid my hands on his chest and closed my eyes. *Please, help him. Do something for him.* Pleading, I cried.

"I need him. Help him," I whispered.

Where the Third was coiled around my arms, warmth was building. I opened my eyes, and through my tears, I saw the Third glowing, the soft blue light washing over Cain as part of the Third slithered down my arms and stretched across Cain's chest. Three offshoots of the Third reared up then plunged through the fabric of Cain's shirt and sank into his flesh. His pale skin took on the blueish tint of the Third, and within moments, Cain gasped, his eyes snapping wide open.

I bent over and wrapped my arms around him. "Thank you," I sobbed over and over again. As a wave of dizziness washed over me, for an instant, I saw the expanse of a glowing sea, the darkness of beaches. And off in the distance, the light brightened until it raced forward like a sizzling branch of lightning and the sea was torn in half.

Emotions of pain and despair rode the heels of the lightning, ripping through me. I looked down at where the Third had touched Cain and noted how it'd lost its light. Bits and pieces of it crumbled as I pulled back, as if it had been burned and turned to ash.

You didn't do that when you healed me. But then again, my injuries hadn't been as severe as Cain's. I hadn't stopped to think about any consequence to what the Third could do. *Thank you for your sacrifice.* I stared at what remained as it coiled itself around my arms once more.

As Cain sat up and stared at me, I felt the aftertaste of sorrow. Whatever the Third was, I knew in that moment that I would help it.

"What did you do?" Cain asked, incredulous.

I shook my head. "I didn't do anything. It was the Third. It… healed you."

"But how?"

I sat back on my heels and shrugged. "I'm not entirely sure, but a theory is beginning to come together."

Before I could elaborate, the ground exploded next to us.

"Move!" Cain roared as he sprang to life. Whatever time Miles had given us was over.

Back to full strength, Cain pulled me to my feet and shoved me forward. We were only a heart-pounding few minutes away from the Spire. Ignoring the pain in my legs, I ran the fastest I'd ever run in my life, and that was saying something.

We ducked under the cover of the Spire as the ground erupted all around us. I pulled Cain over to where the platform had taken me down into the bowels of Dar, praying it didn't need a trigger other than us standing on it to move.

We began our slow descent as the guards continued to fire around the Spire. *Thanks, universe, for lending a helping hand.*

"Your gamble seems to have paid off," Cain commented.

I grinned then caught sight of something moving in the dark. "Holy Jupiter. Cain." I pointed, and Cain's mouth dropped open as he realized what I'd seen.

His tail—the Third had regrown his tail.

Cain's eyes gleamed, and his tail twitched overzealously, which relieved me about his mental state as the platform slowly delivered us downward. As I watched his tail and grinned like a fool, I realized what else might have been healed.

<Cain? Can you hear me?> If the Third had physically healed him—incredibly, he'd gotten his tail back—then the areas of his brain involved in our telepathic communication should've healed as well.

His tail stopped moving, and Cain nodded. "I can."

<And? Come on. Can you respond?>

We came to a stop before he responded. He stepped off the platform, and I caught a slight hitch in his shoulders, and Miles's warning came rushing back. The Third had healed his physical injuries, but perhaps an emotional component was involved, which hadn't healed yet. Or he didn't want to communicate telepathically.

As I followed him off the platform, I grabbed his hand and forced him to turn and face me. "That's okay if you don't want to or you still can't. I understand, and I'll wait. However long it takes. Right now, we focus on helping your sister and getting out of here."

I caught a tinge of amber in his eyes before he squeezed them shut and nodded.

"Alright. It's this way," I said and took a step to the right. But the Third sprang from the earthen walls, coming together to form a barrier.

I should've seen that coming. While the Holy One had implied a grateful and reverent attitude toward the Third, I had sensed an undercurrent of disdain and gotten the distinct impression she hadn't liked being told what to do, especially regarding allowing outsiders. So the question was whether the Third was stopping us or the Holy One and her network of Darquets were asking or even demanding the Third stop us.

"I wonder if the relationship is as symbiotic as it appears," I mused.

"Explain," Cain said.

I looked down at my arms. "Clearly, the Third provides an enormous benefit to the Darquets." When he stared at me, I huffed. "Healing and all?"

"You believe what happened wasn't unique to... us?"

"No," I said. "Look."

I hadn't tumbled to the idea when I was down there the first time, but after seeing the Third heal Cain, I believed I'd figured out the Darquets' little secret. I pointed at a section of the earth where the Third had worked its way through a rocky outcrop.

"Have you ever seen a heart stone?"

Cain snorted. "No. I listened to my father's stories and my grandfather's. But the law forbids any pictures or reproductions in any medium of what they look like. We're taught it's one of our most sacred items to protect."

"I'm seeing why."

Cain reached out and lightly touched the stone. "As a child, I never questioned the stories. Which is why I suppose I—"

His hand dropped, and he turned away to stare at the Third blocking our way.

"Cain?" <*What is it?*>

"Nothing. We need to find a way through this." He spun around and moved down the tunnel in the opposite direction. "This might circle around."

I trailed after then stopped beside him. "When I was down here before, it looked like there might be something metallic down there. Maybe a part of the Spire?"

When I took a step forward to get a better view, something popped and sizzled. "Son of a—" I jumped back and rubbed my nose.

"I didn't think the Third would hurt you?" Cain asked suspiciously.

"It isn't the Third," I said, waving a hand. "No webbing or anything. That's another damned force field."

Cain frowned and took a step closer, his head moving from side to side then tilting back as he studied the opening. "I don't see any projection hubs for a force field. Whatever it is, it must extend into the earth itself."

Still smarting at the sting to my nose, I glared at the opening. "A little warning sign would have been helpful. You know, for tourists that get loose and whatnot."

Cain ignored me. "But why? Why have shielding down here?"

"To keep something in?"

"Or something out." Cain twisted back around. "Look."

"Huh." The soft glow of the Third stopped inches from where the shielding began. As I peered into the space beyond, I realized it was the glow from the Third on the outside that had reflected off the metal. The rest was shrouded in darkness, which didn't give me a good feeling.

"Ever seen anything like this?"

"No," Cain said, wonder in his voice.

The only way I can describe its shape—from what I could see, the thing stretched up and disappeared into part of the earthen wall—was as if some kid had randomly dug a funky hole in the earth then poured hot liquid mercury inside to create a randomly shaped blob. But as I studied the metallic surface, I squinted and leaned forward as far as I could without earning another burn mark. Etched on its surface were thousands of tiny spirals and lines.

"What else do you know about the heart stones? Or the Holy Ones? Where they came from or how they originated?" I asked, turning a sharp eye toward Cain.

"Not much."

"Did you ever sneak in some off-the-record learning about Dar?"

"Of course I did. I went through a phase of trying to find everything I could. But you haven't met my mother. She was thorough. The best I could do was a few popular books and old travel brochures that were easy to source on the net."

Before I could respond, the ground shook, and dirt rained down. Despite being so far underground, I could hear faint voices shouting at each other. I inched my way back to where the platform had stopped and cautiously peeked skyward. I could sense movement and more voices up there, extremely angry voices.

Whatever grade of weapon the Darquets above were using, they were having an effect down below. Perhaps that was what so much of the yelling was about. *Would the Holy One really allow an assault on the secrets buried down here?* Or perhaps our presence in this sacred space was enough to warrant stopping us by any means necessary.

I was surprised no one had rappelled down the tunnel and shot us yet. But centuries of myth and religious belief could cause powerful reactions even in the most motivated people.

"Cain, I don't think we've got very long," I said, glancing at him to find he wasn't paying attention. "We need to figure out how to get past the—"

My eyes rested on the shape in the earth that had derailed Cain's attention.

"My God," I whispered.

23

Ghosts

A xenologist has the choice of which subschooling route to specialize in. My father had instructed my brother and me in all of them. Physical xenology hadn't been my strong suit as a kid. I'd preferred cultural xenology.

When Pops taught us physical xenology, he would show us various bones and ask us to document our steps in how we identified which species it belonged to. Then, we'd have to break down biological sex and any other characteristics we could deduce. Humans typically fall in the middle of the easy-to-hard scale on identification, but not everything is as cut and dry with other species. For some, no skeletal features differentiate between sexes. For others, it's far easier than identifying human remains.

I knew nothing about identifying Darquet skeletons because my father hadn't included them in our studies. But judging by the bits and pieces of flesh still attached to the eyeless face staring at us, I would've hazarded a guess and said it was female.

And nestled under the decaying body's chin was a heart stone.

There's so much to say, but Pops, I can tell you I'm grateful for your lessons. He'd never shielded Lucas and me from the reality of death. I couldn't say how many skeletons I've seen or watched my father uncover, but I could remember the heavy conversations that came from his work on a couple of mass graves where he'd been called in to help identify the victims.

The first time I ever saw a skeleton, its eyeless sockets staring up at me from its grave in the Forlorn Deserts of Ji'oth-Iop, I'd felt faint, and my stomach rolled. But my father had knelt beside me and, in a soft voice, reassured me and started discussing the natural processes of the universe. All life must die, and death can be the seed for new life. He hadn't forced me to stay with him but had encouraged me each day to consider the spark of life that had been tucked away in those skeletons.

The stories he spun about the day-to-day activities of each person, long lost to the tides of history, had sparked my imagination. And in time, I wasn't afraid to gaze upon the bones of those who'd died. Instead, I viewed them with heartfelt sympathy, knowing that, at some point, they'd loved and hated, laughed and cried, just as I did.

Just like the Darquet who was staring back at me. I wondered what her life had been like and how long that place had been her tomb. I wasn't liking this dimension added to the theory I'd formed.

Half a meter to my right was another heart stone. I reached out and brushed some of the dirt away, observing how the Third had pushed through on one side but didn't appear to exit anywhere else. I checked the other one and noted the same thing. *Easier to harvest.*

Above the second stone, I scraped away a thick layer of the earth, and my fingers brushed against something solid. Taking care, I gently finished removing the last layer of dirt and exposed another skull. That one must've been in the earth far longer, as no bits of flesh were hanging off it.

"Do you know Darquet funereal practices?" I asked quietly. "There wasn't mention of anything about them in what I've read."

When Cain didn't answer, I turned to face him.

His skin was as pale as a ghost.

"Cain?"

He stood there, his gaze transfixed to the skull. I wiped my hands on my pants and moved to block his view. *<Cain?>* When he didn't answer, I reached out and gently touched one side of his face. My touch startled him, and he jerked back.

"We... They..." He stumbled over his words. "Cremation is standard practice. They store the ashes of the loved one in the family lineage casket. So the family can find peace together."

"Nothing about burial? Or burial for those who are held in high authority?" I asked.

Cain shook his head. "That would be... sacrilegious." He clenched his jaw, and his eyes found mine. The haze of shock was wearing off, and the years of IGJ training took over. "Darquets revere—no, worship—the earth. It's sacred space to them. Which is why their cities are in the sky, in order to reduce the risk of contaminating the earth with their impurity."

"That would track with what we've learned," I murmured.

"There's so much I don't know. But the one thing I'm sure of is that burying a Darquet is considered anathema. No self-respecting child of Dar would dare place something so unworthy in the earth, no matter their status."

"You're sure?"

Cain growled, and his tail lashed back and forth. "I'm sure. My mother might hate Dar, but there are some traditions that even she can't escape. My father was nearly full-blooded human, and his remaining human relatives wanted his body interred at their family burial site. But my mother wouldn't hear of it. She used the power she had in her office and ordered my father's remains to be cremated."

<I'm sorry. But thanks for sharing that with me.>

If burying their dead was so abhorrent to them, I wondered what those bodies were doing there. My initial theory shifted, and I didn't like the implications.

The ground shook again, with a little more force, and a few seconds later, what sounded like thunder rolled through the air. We glanced at each other, but before we could do anything, another shock wave rolled through the tunnels, then a third and a fourth.

Dirt rained down around us, and Cain grabbed me and yanked me back just in time to avoid a large section of the dirt wall tumbling down before us. Heart stones and bones fell in a jumbled mess at our feet.

Numerous skulls stared up at us. Admittedly, my father's training and the horror show in the *Rapscallion* aside, that was a bit too much.

Whatever shock Cain had felt was gone. "Those aren't Darquet missiles."

With the shock of the skeletons, I'd briefly forgotten about the battle raging above us—not the Darquets who'd charged after us over the house-napping incident, but the larger battle of the IGJ breaching Darquet-controlled space.

"They wouldn't dare," I said. "Would they?"

"In cases of extreme emergency, the Commandant of the InterGalactic Justice system has the express authority to make unilateral decisions. That office is authorized to complete their mission through any means possible. All command decisions will be unanimously approved after said engagement."

I'd forgotten I'd taken up with a walking encyclopedia. "I've never heard that law before. Feels a bit… unethical."

"You wouldn't have," he said. "Can you imagine how the public would react if they knew the IGJ could walk in and do whatever they want?"

I raised my hands to shield my head as another missile impact showered us with dirt. "No, I can't. And I won't ever be able to if we don't get out of here. They keep bombing this area, and the whole thing is likely to collapse."

"But how do we get out? We're blocked on all sides," Cain said.

"No, we're not."

I sprinted over to the barrier the Third had created. We had no time to think, and my whole gesture was going to be one huge gamble. But I was willing to bet it all—and in fact, I was—that my hunches were going to play out.

I lifted my arms, which were still coated with what was left of the Third. "This is what's broken, right? You've been forced to stay down here, serving the Darquets, healing them and who knows what else. But you weren't meant for this, were you? Somehow, you were broken or were separated from where you were supposed to be, and you crashed on Dar.

"Help me now, and I promise I will help you. I'll figure out your truth, what you're searching for. Even if it kills me."

That was a little over the top, but with the walls literally closing in around us, I thought a huge life-or-death gesture should be allowed.

Light burst from the Third wrapped around my arms as it moved to touch the Third blocking our way. The light expanded and grew, and flashes of images bombarded my mind.

The endless sea of light.

The dark beaches, stretching off into the sunset.

Embers of glowing blue light dotting the beach.

Curiosity, isolation, survival.

Joining, longing, renewal.

The Third grew as bright as the sun then winked out as it retreated into the dirt, and the piece from my arm which had connected slid back to curl around my wrist.

"Thank you. I will keep my promise."

I turned toward Cain. "Come on. We don't have much time." Then I sprinted down the tunnel to the cavernous chamber.

The three Darquets I'd seen before were in the same positions I'd left them in, but flecks of dirt had coated their skin and hair. It reminded me of the little flecks of sanctified dirt the Bawthares cooked with. And as a nervous giggle left my mouth, Cain raced past me.

"Elea?" he asked as he moved around the pedestal, gazing up at each face. "Where is she?" He looked over at me, and for the first time, I saw a scared little boy looking back.

"She's here," I said, joining him, and I pointed.

Cain reached out, his hands hovering near her back, but he suddenly stepped back and turned around. "You should be the one to do it. Help her. I'll find a way out."

And without another word, Cain turned to leave.

24

We All Have to Eat, Right?

I understood that the world was literally collapsing around us, but I wasn't about to let Cain go. When I was emotionally wrung out on the *Whimsy*, he'd found me, stayed with me, and comforted me. And I was learning that running away from the things that frightened us the most wasn't helpful.

<*Stop.*>

I put every ounce of emotion, love, and concern I could muster into that single word, and it had the desired effect.

Cain froze.

<*Turn around.*> I was surprised that he did as commanded. But then again, I wasn't. All I was concerned about was him and what he was trying to run away from.

"Look at me," I said. When he didn't lift his eyes, I repeated, <*Look at me.*>

Reluctantly, he did, and his cheeks were wet, his eyes a dull violet.

I closed the distance between us and wrapped my arms around him. At first, he just stood there, his arms hanging limp at his sides. Then, he returned the hug and squeezed hard, so hard that I had to break up the moment. "Um... can't breathe."

Cain released his grip and stepped back. He turned his head and wiped at his face. I sympathized with his embarrassment. During my year of vacation with the IGJ, they'd taught me the weakness of tears. But as Cain, the rascal, was growing on me—and frankly, he was pushing me to grow—I was realizing that tears weren't weakness but a symbol of trying to be strong for too long, and also that tears served a very healthy emotional purpose. To grieve and pay respect to the things lost was healthy and something too many cultures ignored.

"Talk to me," I whispered. "You haven't run from my family's past, and I won't run from yours."

"But you haven't done anything wrong."

The words stung, I had to admit, more than I could've anticipated. I sensed an implication that he'd followed me only because he believed I was one of the good guys. *But what if I wasn't? What if I succumbed to whatever madness had taken over my father and my brother? Would Cain just leave me because it wasn't me he was attracted to but some idealistic vision of whom he perceived me to be?*

My ego raised its vicious little head, wanting to fling back something equally hurtful. After years of maintaining my defenses and being emotionally invulnerable, I had several responses screaming to be spewed at him.

But I didn't want to. That's not what trust was about—or partnership or anything else the two of us were working on.

Instead, I swallowed my instincts and said, "You

didn't do this to her. Obviously, there's a lot of misinformation about the heart stones. But even if there wasn't, it still doesn't mean you're responsible for this." I reached out to brush a lock of hair from his face. The longer hair needed to stay.

"It's not that. I—" Cain looked over at the still form of his sister. With a heavy pause, he seemed reluctant to finish. But he took a deep breath and looked away from the pedestal. "I know Elea would have tried to come here anyway. She was headstrong, more like our mother than either wanted to admit. But after our mother discovered what Elea had done, she refused to do anything to help her. Nothing. No diplomatic immunities or reaching out through back channels. Her hatred for Dar turning its back on our family outweighed her love and obligations as a mother. So I went and pleaded with the only other person I thought would help."

I sucked in a breath as the pieces fell together. "Miles."

"I told him where Elea had gone, why she had left. I thought he loved her, that he could use his authority as the heir apparent to help her before they arrested her. But the next thing I knew, our family received a communiqué from Dar, stating the authorities had arrested and sentenced her."

Cain looked at me, emerald and black mixing in his eyes in a potent combination of self-loathing. "No one should have known. Physically, Elea could pass as a full-blooded Darquet, and at the time, the authorities weren't as strict as they are now. There weren't any blood tests being done to confirm true lineage. That didn't come until a few years later."

"So you believe Miles tipped off the authorities? Why?"

"To get out of the vows he'd made." Cain shrugged then sighed. "We know Miles is always working multiple angles to serve his own agendas. He can't be trusted."

I agreed that Miles was a slippery little eel, full of cunning and plans within plans, but I suspected a layer of decency was still tucked away inside him.

"And you've been blaming yourself this whole time?" I asked.

Cain shrugged. "It's why I joined the IGJ. I'd felt so powerless when all that happened, and I never wanted to feel that way again. And I believed I could one day use my status to help my sister. But the IGJ is an organization that has its issues like any other. And when my rank finally got busted down, I realized trying to help Elea wasn't possible. Until I met you."

"And I was a big enough name, so you stuck around."

Cain reached out and gently laid his hands on either side of my face. "But you must believe me that when I realized you were... my heart's blood, my priorities shifted."

<*I do. No matter where this crazy story takes us. I believe you.*>

Cain released me, leaned forward, and let his head rest on my shoulder. I could feel the hot tears where they fell against my neck. "What if she despises me? All these years, trapped down here because of me," he whispered.

"It isn't your fault. Your sister made her choice, just as your mother did, and Miles. You're not responsible for the actions of the people around you."

"But if I hadn't said anything, then she never would've gotten arrested," Cain mumbled.

"From what I've experienced of Dar, I don't think that's true. Where did you tell her the heart stones were located?"

Cain pulled back and considered the question. "We're told they gift the heart stones to the elder male in each family every seventy-nine years. It's then up to that elder male where and how the heart stone will be stored for the family. I was told the last location of our family's heart stone was in the ancestral Suren home, in the north-east district of Silv."

"But something doesn't quite add up," I said. "Look. Here are the heart stones of Dar. I'm sure of it, since they're connected to the Third, and we know it has the power to heal." I spread my arms to gesture at the glowing lights around us in the cavern.

"Your implication is the heart stones must stay connected to the larger network," Cain said. "Yet the Third you carry wasn't at the time it healed me."

"Good point," I mused. "So what am I missing?"

"Does it matter?" Cain asked. "We need to get Elea and find a way out."

"I know. But there's something here, a piece of the larger picture I need to understand before we leave."

Someone interrupted us. "Clever. Too clever, but I can see why the Third chose you."

I spun around, and Cain moved to stand between

me and the Holy One as she entered the cavern. He crouched, his tail whipping back and forth. I would have swatted it out of the way, but having it back was nice.

"But it didn't choose you," I said, stepping out from behind Cain. He flung an arm out and shook his head to keep me from moving forward.

Sorry, buddy. No can do.

"When you brought me here, you said something about how what lies beneath is not for one such as you. Ergo, the Third didn't actually choose you, or you're just unwilling to sacrifice yourself to it. So—what? You force it to work for you?" I pointed at the Third wrapped around her body.

"Sacrifices must be made. On the part of Dar and the Third."

"You can wrap the idea up into pretty little bows all you want, Holy One, but the truth of the matter is you've taken a sentient life-form and subjected it to a life of servitude."

The Holy One snarled. "We are its guardians. Protectors. What would happen if anyone outside of Dar knew what the Third truly did for my people? How would others use it? Surely, you understand what's at stake."

"Oh, I do. Believe me. Maybe even more than you. This is what my father wanted to study, isn't it? The heart stones or some cultural tradition close enough to the concept that he could get a glimpse of what was going on behind the curtain?"

The Holy One smiled, and the Third shivered where it was visible on her skin. "Yes. Of course. Secrets so many have come close to finding. I would have permitted your father to come to Dar but misguided his research, left him satisfied that he had been mistaken. Something I should have done with the cursed Dr. Ashter."

Oh, no. She did not just imply the man straight-up lied to me. He'd said he couldn't come to Dar because he'd reached the limit of gene-mods. But I bet it was because he knew the Darquets would go after him. *<You're my new mental sticky note keeper. Dr. Ashter has some explaining to do.>*

"And now? What are you going to do with us? Kill us to protect your secret?" I snapped.

Her smile grew vicious and predatory, and the Third stretched across her face like cancer. "Kill you? No. But you will spend the rest of your time in service to the Third, an honored position. You should be grateful. Future generations of Darquets will thrive because of your sacrifice."

Yeah, I don't think so, lady.

<Get Elea. I don't care how you have to do it. Just get her and be ready to run.>

Cain nodded while he slowly backed up.

"I won't be like you," I said, creeping to one side, trying to get the Holy One to follow me and put Cain behind her.

"Oh, you won't." She laughed.

I blinked then almost gagged. "You never told me how Elea secured such an important place in Darquet society."

"A concession, but one that has been made before."

"I bet."

Cain made it to the edge of the pedestal, and I

needed to kill two birds with one stone, to make sure the Holy One stayed focused on me, and to see if I was right.

I raced to the side of the cavern and began tearing dirt away above one heart stone after another. I heard a gasp of shock from the Holy One and glanced over my shoulder. *Perfect—well, in that I'd definitely captured her full attention, but not so perfect, from the murderous expression on her face.*

"How dare you desecrate the Third!" she screeched.

"Lady, I'm not the one who did the desecrating. You are." I jumped over to another heart stone then another and another. *Come on. Prove me right.* I pulled down the dirt above the next stone and almost crowed in delight.

Staring at me was the half-decayed face of a Neetho. I'd gotten lucky. A pure biological Neetho had no bones. They were invertebrate, and any biological tissues would've decayed along with the skin, collapsing the Neetho structure and making it hard to identify. But Neethos had taken to the idea of enhancing their bodies with various types of artificial bone structures—a type of wild plastic surgery for them—stretching their bodies into various shapes.

Thank Jupiter, that particular Neetho had done so, making it easy to identify, and underneath the rotting skin was a metallic bone structure. But more than that, because the individual still carried a large amount of flesh, the Third was wrapped around it, its pulsating blue light giving the entire scene a nightmarish quality.

"The Third has to eat, right?" I said, stepping away from my discovery. "But it just can't be the likes of you or anyone else you deem worthy, which explains why

Elea ended up in a place like this. And why a Neetho would be here. How many other species are buried in this place to keep the Third alive to do your bidding?"

The Holy One stepped back. "It must be done. What better way to pay for their crimes than to give life, to give hope to Dar?"

I wanted to march up to her and kick her or something. Nobody could justify what they were doing there.

But I wasn't the one to get the satisfaction of giving the Holy One her just desserts.

More's the pity.

25

An Unexpected Escape

Cain had wrapped his arms around Elea's waist and lifted her off the platform. The moment her connection was severed, she changed from a perfect statue to a crazy, wild woman. She kicked and flung her hands behind her, trying to find something to grab. Her mouth opened as though she was screaming, but no sound came out. The Third writhed and twisted around her arms and legs.

"Cain, be careful!" I shouted.

The Holy One whipped around, and the Third flew from her body like lightning. It wrapped itself around Cain's legs, and if the situation hadn't been so life and death, his expression of surprise would have been priceless. In all fairness, I'm sure my astonished look was hilarious too. The Third exploded out from my body also and tangled itself with the Third from the Holy One. Together, they writhed around until a tangled mess of knots formed around Cain's legs. I had no way to tell which had come from me and which from the Holy One. I only hoped that was a sign my Third was on our side.

Unable to move or maintain balance, Cain toppled to the ground, freeing Elea. I expected her to race back to the pedestal, to that unknown force keeping her tethered there in mind and body.

She didn't. Instead, she crouched in a posture of midflight, frozen in place. The parts of the Third fighting over Cain unwound from his legs, with thin strips darting and attacking each other. It reminded me of a den of snakes, an unpleasant correlation. I hated snakes.

The Third fought itself, strange shapes and configurations rearing up, each trying to swallow what the other part had made. The Third embedded in the earth rapidly pulsed, and I wondered if it was cheering for either side. I wasn't sure I could translate what I was seeing into human behavior. The Third could be cheering itself on or screaming in anguish. Its actions could be the result of an inane biological behavior, ignorant of what was going on around it. Those fascinating xenology questions would have to be tabled for a later conversation.

The pulsing grew stronger and faster until it appeared to be a steady light, strong enough to illuminate the staggering scope of the cavern. Elea and the two other Darquets on the platform collapsed, their bodies twisting and jerking as if in the clutches of a violent seizure.

Cain crawled over to his sister and sat beside her, watching, unable to help. The Holy One screamed pure rage and lunged for me.

I caught the movement out of the corner of my eye but didn't have time to move far enough away to avoid her. Her fingers caught my arm and snapped me forward.

I tried to throw a punch, but the Holy One used the momentum and flung me to the ground.

I hit hard, and pain exploded across my back. The Holy One fell on top of me, her fingers wrapped around my throat, and with a strength I hadn't expected, she squeezed.

At first, I tried to force my hands between her arms to break her grip, but she was too strong. Pure white eyes stared at me with absolute hatred as she squeezed harder. I clawed at her hands and tried to kick my legs, desperately needing to take a breath.

"You'll destroy us all," she hissed. "You were to be judged guilty, to be taken into the embrace of Dar as all the rest of those who break our laws or threaten our security will do. Why would it choose to let you live?"

If I hadn't been on the verge of passing out, I might have formed a pithy retort. But the only thing I could think of was to jam my thumbs into those hateful eyes.

She screamed with pain and let go. I rolled off to the side, gasping for air, trying to focus. As I pushed myself up, trying to put distance between the two of us, a pair of hands wrapped themselves around the Holy One's neck and snapped the woman backward.

A thank you to Cain was on the tip of my tongue when I realized it wasn't him. It was Elea, and her skin was coated in the Third, but not just her skin. Thick, twisting ropes of the Third stretched down from the ceiling, all coming to connect and spread across her back, up her shoulders, and down her arms. It engulfed her in a brilliant blue haze as the Third moved over her, and tendrils wrapped itself around the Holy One while larger pieces reared up, their edges jagged, then struck. They pierced the Holy One's head, neck, and several locations down her spinal cord and abdomen.

Elea released her grip, and the Third lifted the Holy One off the ground. I thought it had killed her, but after a moment, she tilted her head back and lifted her arms, and the Third placed her on the pedestal to join the other two Darquets, who'd risen and resumed their positions. Arms and gazes lifted once more toward the distant ceiling.

"Elea?" Cain called out hesitantly.

She turned to face us, her skin pale but her eyes a shining amber as she gazed upon her brother.

"Turen, is it… really you? Or another dream?" Her voice was dry and rough. And as she took a step toward her brother, her body trembled.

Cain rushed to her and flung his arms around her. "It's me. It's really me."

They hugged and cried, and as my wave of adrenaline dissipated, I realized we shouldn't have been celebrating yet. But I certainly wanted to toss some confetti and hang some balloons and banners. Cain had found his sister, and she was free.

"Hey, I hate to break this up, but we've still got a problem," I said.

They turned to face me, each refusing to let go of the other.

As dirt continued to rain down upon us, I pointed skyward. "I don't think the action up top has let up. But our chances of survival are greater up there than down here," I said. "I'd really prefer not to be buried alive."

Elea glanced up and shivered, hesitation on her face. "I haven't been above since—"

Cain squeezed his sister's hand. "We'll be with you every step of the way," he said softly. "But she's right. We need to go now."

When we reached the platform, another wave of dirt showered us. I lifted a foot to step onto the platform and raised my hands to cover my head as more dirt rained down.

Then Elea screamed, "Look out!"

The tunnel walls leading us to freedom had taken as much pounding as they could, and they collapsed. Dirt, rocks, and bones dropped all around us, and before I had the chance to jump back to safety, I was buried alive.

Dirt filled my mouth and plugged my nose. Somewhere inside my mind, a voice told me not to take deep breaths, but the primal need for oxygen outweighed any sound thinking. I clawed at the dirt, trying to dig my way out, but I was soon choking and gagging, and my world went black.

My mind fell into a comforting and familiar darkness. Off in the distance, a hint of light appeared, and stretched out before me were the endless undulating hills of darkness. My awareness wasn't totally lost in that impossible place this time, and a part of me knew I should be in pain, that I should die right about then.

But pinpricks of the soft blue light emerged from the darkness and danced all around me. I smiled and watched with rapt fascination as the light came together to form a rather excellent imitation of myself.

The experience was impossible, for a part of me felt

the dirt on my skin, in my mouth and down my throat, but I was also there, in that unknown but familiar place.

Curious, I tried to tilt my head to the side and found that I could in that strange place, and my blue-light reflection did the same.

"Join. Protect. Renew." The words my reflection spoke weren't really words, yet I understood. But where its mouth should have moved, to aid in its speech, the light moved to form a distinct pattern each time.

"Who are you? What are you?"

It reached out to touch my forehead, and the sky broke open. Light poured down around us, and I heard someone calling my name in the distance. I blinked and tried to shield myself from the light, noting my reflection moving away.

"Stop. I need to understand. I still have questions," I tried to say, but instead of words, dirt rolled around in my mouth and mixed with my saliva. The taste was horrid.

"Mahia, hold on," the distant someone called out.

But I didn't want to leave that place, not yet. I was on the verge of understanding what was happening, of finally getting some of the bigger questions answered.

My reflection shifted, and I heard those three words again—*join, protect, renew*—as the not-me twisted into the same patterns that had been etched upon its mouth.

I tried to move toward it, but dirt poured down through the crack in the sky. Giant hands reached down, grabbed my arms, and pulled.

I coughed and choked, spilling dirt from my mouth, and someone hit me on the back. "That's right. Just cough it out. Come on, cough."

"Bad timing," I sputtered.

"If we had been a few seconds earlier, we all would've been buried. So for you, great timing," Cain said as he brushed dirt from my face and hair.

"Not what I meant, but thanks," I said then coughed more. When the fit passed and I felt like I'd dumped a bucketful of Bawthare spice down my throat, I tried to take stock of our surroundings. Our only exit was gone. *Just fudging fantastic.*

"Not quite how I saw myself dying," I muttered. "Really thought I would get shot or blown up. Probably by Miles."

"We will not die here," Cain said. "I won't allow it."

I burst out laughing then regretted it as I coughed up another dirt ball.

Elea spoke. "You won't. They will not allow it."

I wiped my mouth and twisted around to look at her. "I'm Mahia, by the way."

She gave me an absentminded nod. "Yes. I know."

I frowned. "Was I buried that long?"

Cain shook his head. "No. She just seems to know… a lot."

That would make sense. "She was connected to the Third for a long time. I know it can communicate as a collective, and I'm sure it taps into the telepathic abilities some Darquets can exhibit."

"You are correct, Mahia Orion," Elea said. "A living connection, to a telepathic network, had to be maintained in order for Darquet to communicate with the Third."

"That's great," Cain said, "but we need to get you

medical attention. Once we're back on the ship, Dr. Kell will see to you."

"Provided they survive," I muttered. I really hoped we were winning up there but wondered which side Dar would fight on.

Cain helped me to my feet, and I was grateful for the support.

"If the *Samaritan* doesn't make it, then we'll steal a ship and—"

I was watching Elea as Cain was speaking. She turned her back to us and walked farther down the tunnel, opposite the cavern.

"Hey, I wouldn't if I were you," I called out. "The force field packs quite a—"

But Elea moved past it and reached out to touch the metal.

"Well, Jupiter's moons. The fighting must have somehow knocked out the hubs for the field," I said.

"You okay?" Cain asked, and when I nodded, he went to his sister.

In that moment, I did feel a twinge of jealousy. Cain had been reunited with his sister, something he'd dreamed and hoped for. And I was fairly certain Elea had as well. But a joyous sibling reunion wasn't in the works for me. I wasn't looking forward to seeing Lucas face-to-face. Even if he hadn't gotten sucked down a mentally cuckoo wormhole.

But right then wasn't the time to dwell on what I couldn't control.

I stepped up behind them. "Any ideas?"

"Yes," Elea said. What was left of the Third on her

skin wiggled and glowed and slid down her fingers, tentatively touching the metal.

Projecting emotions onto other species is easy when one isn't sure whether they act or behave in similar patterns. But I would've sworn the Third touched the metal, reared back as if in shock or fear, then tentatively stretched out to touch it again—almost as if it couldn't believe it, that some sort of cosmic joke was being played on it. *I feel you there, buddy, believe me.*

When the Third realized nothing was hindering its ability to connect with the metal, it fanned out across the surface, filling the unique patterns etched there. The blue light of the Third penetrated the metal until it took on an eerie sheen. And as the Third spread its light throughout the gloom, I realized what the piece of metal was.

Son of a... It was a ship.

26

Endings and Beginnings

"Well, will you look at that." I whistled.

Maybe the universe was deciding to give me a hand a little more often. I was perfectly fine with that. I thought its IOU list was far longer than mine.

"Elea," Cain said, a note of concern in his voice.

A blank look crossed her face. The Third was all but gone from her body. Only a little remained, spread across her arms and down to where her fingers still touched the ship's exterior.

White eyes turned to stare at me.

"Sacrifice. Trust. Promises."

I didn't like where that was heading.

"There's got to be another way," I said.

"What's happening?" Cain asked. His tail bumped the back of my leg. "What is it doing to her?"

"I can find another way out of here, and I'll be able to keep my promise," I said.

"Incomplete. Journey. Trust."

I bit the inside of my lip, my mind scrambling for options.

"Enough," Cain growled, and he reached forward to pull Elea's hand away from the ship. But the Third reared up and wrapped itself around his hand. Cain tried to break free, and when he couldn't, he started to reach out with his other hand, but I caught it before he could try to rip the Third to shreds.

"It won't do any good," I said.

"You are correct," Elea murmured. She turned to look at us, a flicker of gold within the whites of her eyes. "The Third means no harm to us but must be as it was."

"But there's got to be other options," I said.

"What is it doing to her?" Cain asked with raw desperation.

<*I'm sorry. I really am.*> "The Third needs... what? Something from biological life in order to sustain itself, right? Or else why bury all the bodies?"

"Correct. But it is not the flesh but what the flesh provides that it seeks."

"I hate to break it to you, but I'm not a doctor. No medical sense. You're going to have to explain it a little better than that," I said.

After a hesitation, Elea or the Third—or maybe both—answered. "We do not have adequate experience to describe further. Not all species are suited for our needs, but those who dwell on the surface, who bathe in the light of the stars, provide the bare minimum to sustain our existence."

Elea blinked and looked away. "For generations, Dar has been feeding the Third with those deemed unworthy, a justification made from the twisted belief that this ending is a redemption, that while in life we were not willing to help Dar, in death we can."

"But it doesn't have to be that way with you. You're free. And I'm not asking you to do this." I reached out to gently lay a hand on her shoulder. "There has to be another solution."

The dirt around us shifted, and for a moment, I feared another cave in. But it was the Third, pushing its way through the soil until tendrils broke free to snake toward the ship, adding its light to that of its brethren already curled within the metal etchings.

Elea watched for a moment then turned her focus on Cain. "My time is almost finished. The toll is heaviest upon those chosen to maintain the telepathic connection between the Third and those who believe they are its guardians."

"But isn't that what this is supposed to be about?" Cain asked. "That the Third is used to heal our people? It healed me, and it can heal you." He turned to look at me, desperation plainly written on his face. "Tell her. You're the one who did it. Make it heal her."

"I'm sorry, brother. But this is not possible for me. What one is asked to give cannot be given in return."

"Stop," I said. "The Holy One carried a part of the Third with her. So did I, and it healed me. She told me to ask, and it would be given."

"When the Third chose you, you should have taken my place on the pedestal. But it allowed you to return to the surface. The Third that traveled with you did so of its own free will, which is not how the Holy Ones and those who profess as she does acquire the Third. They forcefully sever a piece of the Third from the whole, to serve as a reminder of what must be sacrificed—not only to those of Dar, but for the Third as well. To remember the power held within and the reason the Third has stayed within Dar."

"But you can come with us. We don't need the Third. Dr. Kell and the others—they'll be able to help you," Cain said then turned his attention to the Third wrapped around his hand. "Please, don't take her from me just when I've found her."

"Brother, I am at peace with this. The Third has been a prisoner, just as I have been. I willingly give myself so it can taste freedom."

"But why?" Cain asked, angry confusion in his voice. "What about us? About coming home?"

"I am home."

"No, you're not." Cain shook his head, tears forming in his eyes. "This isn't home. It never was, and it's all my fault. I should never have told you where the heart stone was. I planted that stupid idea in your head."

Elea smiled. "No, brother, you did not. I had already decided before you told me of its location. My actions were mine alone. You bear no responsibility."

Cain bowed his head as his tears fell. Elea reached out with her free hand and gently lifted his head. They stared at each other before I tumbled to the fact they were communicating telepathically. I gently let go of Cain's hand and stepped away, afraid of interrupting what they were sharing.

When the moment passed and Elea's hand dropped to her side, the Third released Cain. He stepped closer to his sister and gave her a tight hug, whispering something in her ear.

Tears filled her eyes as he pulled away.

"You shall forever be in my heart as well, brother mine." She turned to regard me. "Do well by your heart's blood. Help her fulfill the promise she's made. Heal what has been severed."

Cain nodded. "I will. I promise."

"Elea," I said, hesitant to interrupt. "Can you help me ask it a few questions?"

"Hurry."

"I understand what it's trying to tell me. That something was taken from it, that it needs to find something in order to be whole. And somehow, this is all connected to the Star Eaters and what everyone has been trying to find and use. But what is all of that, really? Where do I go to get started?"

Elea smiled then grimaced in pain. "You've already started on the path. Finish it. The Third will provide the way."

The last of the Third on her hand moved down her fingers, and as the last strand left her flesh, Elea turned toward Cain. She tried to reach out to him one last time, with a soft smile on her lips, but her eyes rolled back, and she collapsed. Cain reached out and caught her before she crumpled to the ground, and he sat with her, head buried against her neck as he cried.

There are never any words to soothe the loss of a loved one. People fumble and say common platitudes, but none of that means much. Those words function more to comfort the onlookers than the ones who are grieving. All I could do was place a hand on Cain's shoulder, letting my touch be a reminder that he wasn't alone. And I ached for him as I watched the Third spread across the ship, knowing he would never have enough time to say goodbye.

"Cain," I said softly. *<Cain, we need to move away.>*

The ship had begun to shake, and the ground vibrated.

He shook his head and held on tight to Elea's body.

I crouched and wrapped my arms around his shoulders and let my forehead rest upon his back. *<We will mourn her, and we will remember her. Don't let her sacrifice be wasted. She gave her life for you. Because she loved you.>*

<If only we could have had more time.>

His voice was as clear as a bell in my head, and I squeezed him and cried with him.

He released Elea, gently placing her on the ground, and stretched forward to place one last kiss upon her brow. "Goodbye," he whispered. We stood, and as he turned to face me, his eyes shifted from a bold amber to a brilliant emerald with flecks of black.

"Now what?" he asked.

I grabbed his hand and pulled him away from the ship. "Now," I said, watching the impossible, "we wait."

27

A Sacrifice... and a Truce (Maybe)

Whatever type of impossible technology powered the ship, it was awesome to behold. The kickback from the engines reverberated through the tunnel. Again and again, the ship moved up to push against its earthen prison.

I was a tad disappointed that a door didn't appear in the ship's side. I'd thought the Third implied it was going to help Cain and me get out. Instead, we were forced to back farther down the tunnel, and I noted the patterns along its exterior shift each time it pushed against the earth. The Third wasn't changing shape, but the etchings in the metal were changing.

"Cain." I elbowed him and pointed.

Not only were the patterns shifting, but the entire shape of the ship was slowly changing.

"How in the worlds is that possible?" I asked.

"I don't know," he said. "The universe is full of wonders yet to be discovered."

I smiled and shook my head. "Didn't take you for a poet."

He shrugged. "There's a lot you don't know about me." <*But that will change.*>

A delightful shiver ran up my spine, and I couldn't help but grin. "I look forward to it."

Enough lovey-dovey mush for the moment. I needed to stay focused on the ship or whatever type of creation or life I was looking at. The word *ship* didn't fit. And I didn't think any other word out there would do it justice. But our minds are designed to see patterns, to find the recognizable in the unknown in order to make sense of our reality. Thus, *ship* it would have to be.

The nose of the ship, which had been freed, lifted, and then what I thought was impossible happened. The material composing the ship folded over on itself to form a sharp point. Tremors rolled off the ship as it shook the earth and rotated until its tip was pointing skyward. It pushed up, digging out of its prison, continuing to shift and rearrange itself into adaptive designs in order to break free.

Cain and I stepped as far back in the tunnel as we could, but despite the impossibility of the situation, the dirt the ship displaced never threatened to fill the part of the tunnel where we were standing. Nor did the walls shift and threaten to collapse.

I wasn't complaining. That was a situation I was perfectly fine with not understanding, as long as we survived.

What I did want to understand, though, was whether the Third was indeed what everyone had been after. *Had*

Pops and his group taken part in generations of selective breeding in order to do what the Darquets had accomplished? To communicate and control the Third? Was the Third what had been turned into myth and legend and dubbed Star Eater?

I chewed on those ideas, and while I was certain I was on the right track, I knew not everything was fitting together—not yet.

But communicating with the Third had to be more complex than mere telepathy. If that was all that was required, humanity should have solved that years before. While extremely rare, it wasn't completely out of the rule book for a human to have some latent telepathic abilities. I wouldn't have been surprised if I actually did. That would explain why Cain could communicate and build a connection with me and also explain my connection with the Third.

I had a hard time believing that, in all the years and generations of research, no one would have thought of that angle, that my father wouldn't have.

However, what I'd learned didn't answer the question of how the sun crazies had known what to look for and why they'd attempted to develop the smart-bots. A relationship with Dar might've been possible before Dar closed its borders, but that answer didn't sit right with me. I didn't think the purists would want that type of association. And that wouldn't explain why Pops would find it necessary to petition to work on Dar.

All those questions led me to another potential conclusion. Remnants of the Third might exist on other planets, enough that researchers like Pops and Dr. Ashter had a few small clues, but not enough to form a definitive answer. Or perhaps they did and were simply missing what the Darquets had established with the Third. *"Took by force" would be a better description. And does that answer the question of what I'm supposed to heal? That I need to find all the scattered parts of the Third?*

But those ideas only churned out more questions. *If that was the case, why did it need me?* The Third had its ship, or its means of transport, anyway. It was going to break free from the control of Dar. It would stand to reason the Third could go and seek out its own and heal itself.

Cain interrupted my train of thought when he shouted, "Watch out!" as he grabbed my arm, pulled me to him, and used his body as a shield.

The ship had broken free, and a deep rumble filled the tunnel. As it ascended, joy, sorrow, and fear all washed over me. But underneath those feelings was something far more potent: rage.

The last of the dirt coating the ship fell down the newly minted shaft, dancing in the sunlight. I rushed forward, eager to see what would happen next. I didn't get to witness something as crazy as that every day.

In the distance, I could hear weapons fire, and from my vantage point, I could see the tops of the surrounding trees swaying in the wind. The light filling the hole turned a soft yet brilliant blue, and after a massive clap of thunder, the world fell silent except for the sound of my heart just about marching itself out of my chest.

I strained to listen but couldn't hear the battle sounds any longer. Instead, everything was overbearingly silent.

"Think we can climb?" I asked Cain as he joined me.

He eyed the sides of the tunnel with a dubious expression. "I think it's our only choice."

He walked up to the edge and dug his fingers into the earth. He was able to get a meter off the ground before the earth gave way under one of his hands and he fell.

"Maybe not," I muttered. "You okay?"

He stood, shook himself off, and grimaced. "Yes."

I walked over to the opposite side and studied the dirt. No vines or tree roots were available though I wasn't sure those would've been much better. And naturally, we didn't have any equipment with us.

"What about the platform?" Cain asked.

"What about it? It's buried under a mountain of dirt. We would have to clear all that out, and who knows if the tech still works?"

"Worth a try."

It was—a long shot and a very tedious try. But we were out of options. I didn't want to scream my head off for help, not knowing who might hear us. *Except for...*

Sam? Are you there?

I waited but didn't hear a response. So I really was out of ideas. "Fine. The platform," I grumbled.

But as we headed back toward the platform, the dirt along the parts of the tunnel wall still intact shifted. "Cain, look—" I said, afraid of another cave in. But thin tendrils of the Third poked out of the dirt and snaked their way toward us.

"I thought it all left with the ship," Cain said as he slowly backed up.

I stood still and watched. No hint of the blue light showed from its strange exterior.

"I'm guessing most of it did, or at least what could reach the ship. Think about how much of the Third was in the cavern. But look." I reached out and let it touch my fingers. "I think... I think it's dying."

"Are you sure that's wise?" Cain asked. <*I can't lose you too.*>

<*You won't.*>

The Third brushed against my skin then continued to push past me to where the ship had been. Its tendrils moved along the walls and made half-formed patterns as it stretched up toward the surface.

"Come on," I said. "I think it's trying to help."

Cain didn't question me but stepped up and touched the Third, giving it a gentle tug. It didn't move from its position on the wall.

"I'll go first," he said.

Cautiously, he used the Third as a ladder and climbed up out of the hole. When he was halfway up, I started my ascent. That didn't take long, and when Cain was on the surface, he turned around and stretched out his hand for mine. He helped pull me up the rest of the way, and we sat there gaping at what awaited us.

What was left of the spire lay in pieces off to our left, and as far as the eye could see, the grand floating cities of Dar lay in ruins on the planet's surface. Smoke wafted up from the smoldering shards, and when I glanced up into the sky, nothing but fluffy clouds dotted a crystal-blue sky.

When I shifted, pressing a hand to the ground to push myself up, something sharp pierced my skin.

"Ow!" I yelped and pulled away. When I looked down at what had bitten me, I saw a small piece of metal.

Oh no. I reached out and held it up to the light. Parts of patterns were etched on its surface.

"Cain, look," I said.

He didn't respond.

I looked up and saw him staring at the destruction. I hadn't thought about what this would mean to him. "Cain, I'm really sorry. I had no idea it would do this."

He shook his head and looked at me with a blank expression. "Do this?"

I took his hand and placed the piece of metal in it.

"The Third. It destroyed—" Saying it felt impossible, but I forced the words. "The Third has destroyed Dar. I'm sorry. If I'd known…"

Cain swallowed then clenched his jaw as his fingers slowly curled around the piece of the ship.

"What happens when the slave revolts against the master?" he asked.

"Not this. This wasn't the answer to that question. Dar should have been held accountable for its actions, but needless slaughter doesn't heal anything."

He turned and looked skyward. "I dreamed of coming to Dar one day. To walk along its pathways, to have a moment of believing I could belong. But as my sister wasn't able to, neither shall I."

"I'm not sure that's—"

"Should I be concerned about associating with the last sane Orion?" someone called out in a familiar voice. "I mean, this kind of takes the cake."

I scowled and looked off to my right. *Miles.*

"You're the one who set this whole thing in motion," I grumbled as I got to my feet. Cain rose beside me, still gripping the piece of the ship.

Miles stopped and looked down at the hole in the ground. Then he looked at me then at Cain. "Did you find her?" he asked quietly. His shift in demeanor was jarring.

Cain bared his teeth, his tail snapping back and forth. "I did. And no thanks to you, she died in this horrid place."

Before I could react, Cain spun the piece of metal in his hand and brandished it like a weapon. He lunged for Miles, and before Miles could defend himself, Cain cut the side of the would-be emperor's face, a deep wound from the edge of his right ear down to the corner of his mouth.

"Sir," someone called out, concerned.

I realized Miles hadn't been alone. Coming into view was Commander Lio and a handful of other officers from the *Samaritan*.

A few weapons were raised, and I raced over to Lio. No way was I going to physically stop Cain and Miles, not even if I wanted to.

"Stop," I said. "Don't shoot. Let this play out."

Lio threw me a skeptical look but didn't argue.

Cain and Miles separated, both breathing hard and covered in cuts.

"What are you implying?" Miles asked. "You think I wanted this for her?"

"You're the one who told the authorities," Cain snapped and tried to punch Miles. But Miles dodged the fist, rotating, and landed a hard kick to the side of Cain's knee.

"I went to you for help, but Elea was arrested. How else would they have known?"

Miles snarled. "I loved your sister, you little brat. I tried to help, I wanted to help, but my brother threw me in jail, remember? I didn't have a hand in her arrest."

"I don't believe you!" Cain yelled and lunged again.

He collided with Miles, and they fell to the ground. Miles gained the upper hand and pinned Cain to the ground. The filthy scuttle crab had ahold of Cain's tail and was trying to strangle him.

I was ready to intervene and reached out to snag Lio's gun from his holster, but the commander swatted my hand away. Thankfully, Miles stopped at the same moment and leaned back, staring at Cain. "I wouldn't have hurt Elea. Why do you think I changed my mind about the marriage?"

"That's not what you implied earlier," Cain snapped then coughed. He pushed Miles off and scrambled away.

"Brother, how long will it take you to understand I speak in riddles and half-truths? Ingrained habits die hard, you know."

"Well, it's one habit you're going to have to work through," I said, glaring at him.

Miles threw me a wounded look as he gingerly touched the gash on his face. "Perhaps. But only for you."

"Explain," Cain said.

"The family—more to the point, my aunties—implied that if I went through with the marriage, they would make sure Elea wouldn't survive the year. When

I hesitated, they proved their point by poisoning your father. If you want someone to blame, I would look at them. Their rotting corpses, at least. When I escaped my brother's clutches, I paid my aunties one last visit."

"You really are mad, aren't you?" I said.

"More than likely." Miles sighed.

<Do you believe him?> Cain asked.

<Jupiter help me, I do. Even if he's leaving out details, I really don't think he had anything to do with your sister's arrest.>

After a pause, Cain pushed himself to his feet. Miles reached out a hand for help up, but Cain ignored it and came to stand by my side.

<Fine. But he's still a piece of trash.>

28

We Won... Sort Of

"Is that the whole reason you've been out for blood? Derailing glorious schemes and plans I labored over?" Miles asked Cain as we followed Lio and the others.

Cain shrugged, and Miles huffed.

"How did you find us?" I asked.

"We've been trying to reach you, but comms went down shortly after the IGJ engaged us in battle," Lio said. "But it would seem Sam has made it a part of her programming to keep tabs on you."

"Sam?" Cain asked.

"The ship's AI," I said.

He pursed his lips but nodded. "Good."

"Dare I ask who won?"

"Do you think we would be here if we hadn't?" Miles replied.

"Well, things aren't really going to any type of logical plan, so who's to know anymore?"

<You can say that again,> Cain grumbled.

"We wouldn't be here if it wasn't for the Dar military joining the fight. If they had stood by their policies of noninterference, the *Samaritan* wouldn't have stood a chance. They sent three warships to apprehend us."

"Three? Was Yilmaz on one of them?" I asked.

Lio stopped and turned to face me. "No. But she left a message for you."

"Let's have it." I sighed.

"It's on the ship, encoded for your eyes only. Sam won't play it until you're there in person."

Oh goodie, just what I'm looking forward to.

"The shuttle's just up ahead," Miles said. "Come on."

"Wait. What about Dar? Is everything"—Cain swept a hand out toward the smoldering ruins—"like this?"

"No. Scans show whatever the two of you did was contained to this area."

"Hold on. The two of us? You think we had something to do with this?" I asked.

Lio looked embarrassed as he answered. "I was working under the theory you facilitated this, yes."

"And why would you think that?"

"Hold on to your engines, girl," Miles said and stepped toward me. When Cain growled, Miles held up his hands in defeat. "I knew the two of you headed off in this direction, and while most of Dar's military force was ordered to fight the IGJ, we kept tabs on the area. There was a small contingent that followed you." He grinned. "Not to mention we may or may not have tapped into their communications system. It seems like you made quite the impression on the Holy One—so much so she ordered the two of you shot on sight."

That wasn't surprising. "But you haven't answered

my question. Why do you think Cain and I would do something like this?"

"To escape?" Lio offered.

"Did the ship not pick up on anything else? A rather large object that would have appeared just before everything was destroyed?" I asked.

Miles squinted and pursed his lips. "What are you getting at?"

"Nothing." I shook my head. <*Don't say anything. If Sam didn't pick up on the Third, I would rather keep it to ourselves for a bit first.*>

<*I understand.*>

Miles watched us but didn't press.

"Captain, incoming reports," an officer said. "Looks like there's a small battalion of Dar military headed our way."

We took off at a jog and in a few minutes were secured in the shuttle and taking off. The Holy One might not have survived, but she hadn't been the only one controlling the Third. It was safe to assume I could scratch Dar off as an ally.

Lio opened comms to the *Samaritan*. "Are we under attack?"

"No, sir," came the reply. "The temporary cease-fire holds. The IGJ has maneuvered to a higher orbit. Scans show they're powering up overdrive engines. Dar forces are inbound, but weapons are not activated. We are anticipating a time limit on our stay though, sir. We're working to get critical systems ready for departure."

"Cease-fire? I thought we'd won," I asked.

Lio replied, "We did, barely. With the Dar forces,

we crippled the IGJ ships, and they pulled back. Then the"—he glanced away for a moment—"incident occurred planetside. The Dar ships received orders to pull back. We braced for the IGJ to take advantage, but it appears we no longer hold their interest."

No doubt, Yilmaz's message held a clue about what was going on with the IGJ. And though I was tempted to feel relieved that something was distracting them from blowing us up, I almost wished they would've continued fighting. If something else out there was diverting Yilmaz's attention—what I could only describe as a vendetta—from me, then it couldn't have been good.

<I wish you could've had more time. Maybe visited your ancestral home and all.>

Strapped into the seat across from me, Cain closed his eyes. *<Yes. I would've enjoyed that. But this isn't home. It never was.>* His eyes opened and shimmered with a beautiful golden hue. *<My home is now wherever you are.>*

I blushed, and my chest tightened at the thrill laced within those words. We sat in comfortable silence for a time, then I asked, *<Will you contact your mother? Tell her about Elea?>*

For a moment, I wondered if the subject was still too raw as Cain didn't respond. But he finally did. *<In time. To do so now would only raise more questions and attention than we need at the moment. And mother... For her, Elea died the moment she left for Dar.>*

Anguish and frustration filled the connection between us, and I didn't push. In fact, I surely would've responded the same if the positions were reversed.

"So now what?" Cain asked.

I let my head rest against the back of the seat. "We get cleaned up, get a decent meal. Then tackle whatever little goodie Yilmaz left for me. And sleep. I could use a decent night's sleep."

Cain nodded. "Agreed."

We made it back to the *Samaritan* without further incident. Lio was bombarded by two other commanders providing updates, tactical analysis, and reports on the damage to the ship once we docked.

"Where to?" Miles asked.

"I don't care. Just not here."

"Read you loud and clear." He threw a mock salute and went after Lio and the others.

"Shall we?" I turned and asked Cain.

A sly smile spread across his face, and he looked at me with a mischievous twinkle in his eyes. I took that as a strong yes.

We stepped out of the shuttle bay, and I led the way to the quarters I'd been assigned. When the door closed behind us, Cain grabbed me around the waist and pulled me close. Eyes bright, he leaned forward.

[T̶here's an urgent message from Commandant Yilmaz of the InterGalactic Justice System for you. Your eyes only.]

Not now.

[T̶he message is marked urgent.]

With a deep sigh, I pulled back. Cain frowned.

"Hold, please," I said and gave him a quick kiss on the cheek. "Sam isn't going to stop until I hear what Yilmaz has to say."

Cain didn't verbally complain but had an obvious look of disappointment. We headed over to the screen, and I switched on the interface.

"Sam, go ahead. Play the message."

"This message has been marked for your eyes only. Turen ed-Suren will need to leave—"

"Nope. Not going to happen. Whatever you have to do to override the security stamps, do it."

"Processing," the AI voice replied.

<*We finish this together.*>

<*Together,*> Cain thought.

The screen blinked, and Yilmaz's face appeared. "Ah. Ms. Orion. Good of you to respond. And I see you've kept your usual stubborn personality and brought a friend."

Sam, cut it! This isn't a message. This is live feed.

[Unable to complete the request. The system is locked.]

Yilmaz leaned forward. "I'm not sure how you convinced the Darquets to come to your aid, but rest assured I will not let this setback stop me from reaching my goals. In fact, I enlisted the help of an old colleague. He doesn't like to take sides—academic principles and all that. But when someone pins their career on playing to the highest bidder, well... It's amazing, the resources of the IGJ."

"Jupiter's storms," I muttered. "But I don't see how Dr. Ashter is going to be of much help."

"Quite the contrary. He's already been a tremendous help, making headway with the files you sent."

Files? I didn't send any files. Oh, blow it out an airlock. The recordings I'd sent Sam. I'd even enlisted Dr. Ashter's help in deciphering what the Third had been doing.

Sam, where is Dr. Ashter?

[DR. ASHTER IS NO LONGER ONBOARD THE SAMARITAN.]

Curses all around.

Sam, whatever security clearance he had, delete it now. We can't take the chance he can do a remote linkup and get back into our files.

[AFFIRMATIVE. SHALL I FILE A REPORT WITH CAPTAIN LIO?]

Yes. Whatever you need to do. Do it.

"Yilmaz, you need to listen to me. Whatever you think you're chasing after, I can bet you've got the wrong idea. If you're even a shred of what you project to the worlds, a line of defense against the injustices everyone faces, then you need to hear me out."

I felt as slimy as one could get, like I was about ready to make a deal with the devil, to borrow from an archaic saying.

But Yilmaz beat me to the punch. "I care about defending the worlds. But you'll have to pardon me if I'm not ready to take your word on much. They have cleared you of any suspicion after your father's arrest, but with the actions of your brother and, now, what has happened on Dar… Well, I think it best I secure what has captured the attention of so many. And then I will decide how any information or technological advancements will be disseminated."

Fine.

"Then what do you want? To gloat?"

She smiled, a small, annoying smile. "Perhaps. A small touch of ego is involved in contacting you. But I needed visual confirmation of your physical status. Dr. Ashter insisted on that being a condition of his new-found employment."

Yilmaz looked as if she wanted to say something else, but her smile vanished, and the screen went dark.

Cain turned to stare at me, eyes a sparkling emerald. "Your stubborn personality can be a useful trait. But if they needed physical confirmation, then you need to get to medical. Have Dr. Kell run a full spectrum analysis, then we will discuss what to do next. We could try to draw Yilmaz out, set a—"

I couldn't help but laugh. "Cain, I'm a few steps ahead of Yilmaz, at least where my health is concerned. I don't have the smart-bots anymore. Remember? The Third waved its magic wand and, presto chango, replaced them."

"You don't know that for sure. The Holy One could've been lying."

I shook my head. "No, I'm confident on that topic, at least. She wasn't. But I'll go see Dr. Kell if that makes you feel better. The real issues are what Dr. Ashter figured out that I need to. And the sooner, the better."

"I'll agree to that only if Dr. Kell clears you," Cain replied.

"Great. Let's go."

I passed every test Dr. Kell threw at me and even a few more Cain insisted she run, while an assistant checked Cain over as well. I hadn't forgotten the mystical healing that had taken place. As I hopped down off the medical platform, I threw a smug look Cain's way. <*Told you so.*>

His tail twitched, and my grin widened.

As we left medical, Miles was waiting for us, casually leaning against a wall and munching on an apple, of all things. "What's up?"

"Nothing. I just know something Yilmaz doesn't."

Miles straightened up. "Yilmaz? You played the message?"

"Wasn't a message," Cain said. "But none of your concern."

"Actually, it is," I said, which earned a scowl, "but that can wait. I wasn't kidding about being hungry and needing some sleep."

"But—" Miles protested.

"Miles, you can learn to wait," I said over my shoulder.

Cain brooded as we went back to my rooms, and once we had some privacy again, I turned to face him.

"Spit it out," I said.

"How did you know?"

"Intuition?"

Cain huffed. <*Not good enough.*>

"I know. Look, order some food, and we'll talk while we eat."

He didn't like it, given the continual twitching of his tail, but Cain ordered a resplendent feast, and I tried to make sure I updated him on everything, including my visions or hallucinations or memories. I wasn't sure how to categorize them.

We batted ideas back and forth, but by the time I

was finished, my brain was fuzzy, and I was about ready to fall asleep.

Cain stood, walked over, and pulled out my chair. With no warning, he bent over, scooped me up, and walked over to the bed. <*You need to rest.*>

I did. My brain and body needed a chance to unwind and regroup, then I would tackle our next steps. I pressed my head against his chest, enjoying the warmth of his body and the slow, steady beat of his heart. <*Cain, I need you to know something.*>

His grip tightened. <*I already do.*>

I couldn't help my nervous giggle. "But I need to say it out loud." I turned my head to stare at him. "I love you."

The words weren't easy for me to say. I hadn't thought about that depth of sentiment or human attachment for years. I let a hand rest against his chest as he carefully let go so that I could stand.

He bent his head and kissed the side of my neck, his breath warm, sending shivers up and down my spine. "I love you as well."

"Stay with me," I whispered. "I know you said this was complicated for you and you didn't want—"

Cain shifted his weight and pulled me close, and his lips found mine. <*We're past complicated.*>

<*Excellent.*>

29

Itheron and Lia

When I woke up, tangled in a mess of sheets and a handsome former IGJ agent, I couldn't help the stupid grin spread across my face. Careful not to wake a slumbering Cain, I untangled myself and went to the bathroom to freshen up.

That stupid grin wouldn't leave my face as I stared at myself in the mirror. I felt nothing but pure happiness bubbling inside, and I wished the feeling would never leave.

Zipping up the front of a fresh jumpsuit, I stood in the doorway to the bedroom and stared at Cain. *Thanks, universe.*

But as much as I wanted to stay wrapped in the delicious feeling of being loved and loving him in return, I had work to do.

Not wanting to disturb Cain, I left a message on the screen about where I was headed, and I set off for Dr. Ashter's office.

Sam, can you have Miles join me?

[AFFIRMATIVE.]

By the time I reached the office, Miles and Commander Lio were waiting for me. Miles studied me then raised an eyebrow. "Sleep well?"

"Perhaps." The lights flared to life as we entered. "How did Dr. Ashter get off the ship?"

Lio's Telt heritage showed through as visible tufts of fur rose in irritation. "My oversight. I take responsibility."

"I'm not looking for blame," I said. "I'm just curious to know. Do we have any further moles? Or people we can't trust?"

Miles shook his head. "No. I've seen to that."

I didn't care for the sound of that but decided not to press.

"The melting code triggered a cascade that ate its way through all major systems, temporarily shutting them down. For a few minutes, we were blind, with internal and external sensors down," Lio explained.

"And we've determined the source of the melting code," Miles added with a quirk of one eyebrow.

"I know. They attached it to a message from my lawyers. I'd asked Sam to work on it," I replied, nonplussed by his attempt to unbalance my calm. "So how long has Dr. Ashter been double-dipping in credit streams? If Yilmaz sent the code as a distraction for him, then that would imply he's been working with her for far longer than just switching sides when it was convenient."

"A better question is why didn't he just stay on the *Justus*? Far less risky than what he did. Why did he need to come back to the *Samaritan*?" Lio asked.

Miles's gaze darkened. "I paid top dollar for that man—with guarantees, in writing, mind you—that he would work solely for me. This is a major breach of contract. I'll take him for everything he's worth."

"Is that all you can think about? How this is affecting you and your wealth? Or status? This is a lot bigger than the temper tantrums of a man-child," I said.

Miles looked up at me. I expected a quip or demeaning remark for my insult.

Instead, he nodded. "You're right. My apologies."

"Well, that's got to be a first," Cain said as he joined us.

<*I didn't want to wake you.*>

He walked over and gave me a quick kiss on the cheek. <*I could sense when you left.*>

<*Really? Sorry. I tried to be as quiet as I could.*>

He shook his head. <*No, not physically.*> He raised a hand and tapped the side of my head. <*In here. You're going to need to read the myth about Itheron and Lia now.*> Then a wide, mischievous grin appeared, along with a delicious spark of amber in his eyes.

<*I'm moving it up to a priority spot on the to-do list right now.*>

"Oh alright. Enough with the romantic junk. Cut it out, you two," Miles said and rolled his eyes.

"I will for Commander Lio's benefit, not yours," I said with a wink at Lio. I was pleased when he winked back.

I walked over to one of the larger screens in the room, switched it on, and asked Sam to bring up the recordings. "We need to comb through everything Dr. Ashter did, not just his files, but his movements. All his interactions with the crew... and with me. But we also need to figure out what he could've put together from the files I sent to the ship while on Dar."

The screen moved through the images and video Sam had captured, displaying the unique patterns and symbols of the Third.

"I'll let you get to work on that, and I'll start working through his movements on the ship," Lio said. "We also are still cycling through repairs and running out of leeway with the Dar military. We need to break orbit within the hour even if it means we're crawling through space."

Lio moved toward the door. "I want an update in a few hours. Let us break orbit, then talk to me about what you're working on, and we'll see if I can find anything to help understand his motivation."

"Will do." I wasn't sure how much I would share with the commander—scratch that, I needed to update my terminology—the captain. I did trust the Telt, but a part of me knew the time wasn't right to reveal everything about the Third—another intuition thing.

"Right. And I need to do an inventory of my things." Miles held a hand up in a flourish. "Not because I'm materialistic. Well, I am, but that's beside the point. Dr. Ashter had full access to everything Star Eater. I need to make sure of what's here and see if he absconded with anything useful."

I didn't reply, and Miles left with a disappointed look on his face. Engaging in his silly little theatrics wasn't worth my time at the moment. A reckoning would come for the would-be emperor, but not yet.

"I'll grab some snacks, then we can get to work," Cain said.

<How about a big old breakfast? That sounds better.>

"Breakfast it is," Cain murmured. He gave me a rather long kiss before he left, which didn't help my concentration at all.

When the door closed, I turned back to the screen, ready to concentrate. I pulled up a chair and watched the images and videos repeat themselves several times. Working with a handheld screen, I pulled up Dr. Ashter's files and shifted through his notes. Nothing was in there about the files I'd sent. I figured he wasn't dumb enough to leave a clue behind, but it had been worth a look.

Something was very familiar about what I was seeing, but I couldn't place why. Frustrated, I stood up and started pacing, hoping for a light bulb moment of clarity.

Cain returned, laid out the food, and dished up a plate for me. He held it out as I passed, and without thinking, I snagged it and ate as I paced.

"These aren't from the replicator, are they?" I said around a mouthful of hash browns.

Cain grinned. "I figure we're owed the use of Miles's personal chef."

I speared another mouthful and nodded. *You bet your shiny rockets, we are.*

"Just work your way through the different places you were at with your father," Cain suggested. "Start at the beginning. Tell me about them."

I stopped and stared. "How did you know that's what I was considering? I wasn't trying to tell you anything."

Cain smirked as he speared a piece of fried egg. "I told you. Look up the myth."

"Why don't you just tell me?"

Cain grinned, eyes dancing with delight. "Perhaps I should show you instead."

I blushed and was sorely tempted by the offer. *Focus. Stay focused.* "Sam, pull up the Darquet myth about Itheron and Lia."

Sam processed the request, and a long sonnet-type work appeared on the screen. After reading the first few lines, I blushed. "This is..." I glanced at Cain. "Not what I expected from the austere literary minds of Dar."

"You'll find a wide range of literature," he commented dryly. "But this should be most... informative."

I read through the rest of the story, and in summary, Itheron was the son of an esteemed family, destined to take his father's place on the Ruling Council. Darquet marriages are typically arranged through yearlong negotiations with a wide range of suitable families. But Itheron found himself drawn to Lia, who was due to be accepted into the ranks of the Ascended, a position where marriage was deemed a distraction.

After figuring out what the Ascended and the Holy Ones got up to, I could understand why they felt marriage would be a distraction. *Hypocrites.*

Anyway, Itheron and Lia continued to meet, against their family's wishes, and the pair realized they were each other's heart's blood. But Itheron's family wouldn't hear of the union, and neither would Lia's. Itheron was given a bride and a position off world as an ambassador to Kolde.

But because Itheron and Lia had, shall we say, made everything official in their own way, Itheron felt nothing at all for his wife. And Lia had no choice but to flee Dar and search for Itheron as she was drawn to him like a moth to a candle.

"Wait, this implies they have to be physically near each other." I scanned through the rest of the text. "Or else, what? You get sick?"

Cain stood and came to wrap an arm around my waist, his tail curling around my legs. "Yes," he whispered. "Once union is fully shared, emotionally, telepathically, and physically"—he made sure I understood what all that meant—"then the two become one."

"A head's up would've been nice," I mumbled.

<*Are you complaining?*>

<*No. Not really. But I might hold it over you every once in a while.*>

"I look forward to it," Cain murmured and started trailing kisses down my neck.

"Yeah, me too," I said then cleared my throat. "But seriously, what else do I need to know?"

Cain stopped distracting me and sighed. "Our bond will deepen. Rumors suggest we'll have a general sense of where the other is at all times, feeling the other's emotions even more strongly than we do now." He turned me so that I was facing him. "You're not…?"

"No. I'm not regretting anything. It's just a lot to process on top of everything else we've been through in—what? Less than a month?"

He pursed his lips and considered. "It feels longer."

"You bet it does. But if I had to choose someone to go with me on this crazy adventure, I'd choose you anyway. So, no. I'm not regretting a thing. It'll just require some adjustments."

"I suggest we practice right away," Cain murmured. He took my plate and set it on the table, and for a little while, we forgot about anything else.

30

Goodbyes

I gobbled the cold remains of our breakfast, and as tempted as I was to just forget about everything that needed sorting, I forced myself back to the issues at hand. I worked through several years of adventures as a kid, regaling Cain with outrageous stories, but nothing clicked for me.

"You should take a break," Cain suggested.

"Can't. Lio needs an update. And we need to know what Yilmaz is thinking of doing."

"I'm not sure that's entirely possible," Cain replied. "Yilmaz earned her position by outmaneuvering scores of competition for the commandant position, not to mention her years of service within the IGJ and an outstanding record."

I shrugged. "I wasn't up to snuff when she met me. She doesn't know me yet."

Cain grinned. "Good. That's what I want to hear."

Sam's voice broke through. "Attention, Miles High is requesting your presence on Deck Thirteen, Observation Lounge 3A."

"Great, what does the scuttle crab want now?" I muttered.

"Scuttle crab?" Cain asked.

"Too much downtime on our way to Dar. Don't ask. Come on. Let's get it over with, whatever it is."

When we entered the observation deck, the room's lighting had been turned down, and the view screen was on, revealing a breathtaking landscape of Dar and its three moons. Someone had draped silk sheets throughout the rooms, deep purples and vivid greens and blues. Candles were arranged in different clusters along the tables, and a bright-yellow plant had been placed in the center of the room.

Cain hissed and shook his head. "No."

I felt a rush of anger and turmoil inside of him. <*What's wrong?*>

Miles stepped out of the shadows, dressed in a tunic matching the colors of the room. For the first time, I saw him as a part of the monarchy. The gash on his cheek was pink with new flesh, his hair was slicked back, his expression somber, and he carried an air of power, as well as sorrow.

"You've no right," Cain snarled.

As he took a step back, I grabbed his arm. <*Talk to me.*>

But his emotions were all I felt in our connection. So I turned my attention back to Miles. "What is this?"

"A ceremony in remembrance of Elea el-Alea ed-Suren."

<*We don't have to stay.*> I turned back to Cain. <*I'm with you whatever you choose.*>

to turn around, so I followed him.

se," Miles called out.

ed but remained facing the door.

"I know we've had our... differences. You've tried to have me arrested, or worse, numerous times. And I've worked to derail your career in retaliation. And I'm not a good man. I've done terrible things for power and for my own selfish desires. But if there was one thing in my life I regret the most, it's your sister. I truly loved her. She was smart and witty, not unlike the woman you yourself love. She would've made life as emperor bearable."

Cain slowly turned to face Miles as the man spoke. For the first time, I truly believed every single word coming out of his mouth, not sensing any doublespeak or hidden agenda there.

"Please, allow me to pay my respects, to honor her as is befitting her life. Let me give us both a chance to say goodbye."

Tears welled up in Cain's eyes, and I reached out and entwined my fingers with his. <*Let me stand with you. Let us say goodbye and thank her for the sacrifice she made.*>

Cain squeezed my hand, and we walked over to the plant.

<*Yellow zings were her favorite,*> Cain shared.

Miles reached out and let a finger trace the ruffled edge of one of the blooms. "She gifted me with this plant the first time we met. Not because she had any idea what her mother was planning, but simply as a gesture of respect from one person to another. I'm surprised my aunties didn't have it burned, but I suspect excavation and history projects were funded by the monarchy. Interest in religions was a big topic in the family. And I know everyone believed some powerful prize was out there that, if found, would put humanity at the top of the food chain, permanently. But everyone had only bits and pieces of the puzzle. But I knew your father could put it together. Just as I know you will too."

"Oh fudge," I said and sat up straight. "I forgot about Lio."

"Don't worry. I told him the two of you would be indisposed for a while," Miles said. A shadow passed over his face, then an unsettling grin appeared. "I've got work to see to. I'll leave you two alone… for now."

"Before you go, what about Dr. Ashter?" I asked. "What is his stake in all of this?"

Miles's expression darkened. "Fame. Fortune. That's all that man has ever wanted. If he finds what everyone has been looking for, he'll sell the information to the highest bidder. Which I'd believed had been me. But that's twice now the IGJ has outbid me on personnel. I can assure you it won't happen again."

I didn't like the sound of that but wasn't up for an argument. As the door slid shut behind Miles, I twisted to look at Cain. "You okay?"

His eyes were red, but he nodded. "I will be. I'd carried hope I would find her alive, rescue her, and somehow, everything would go back to how it'd been. But that was a foolish dream. We can never go back."

<Funny. Miles was saying something along the same lines.>

I sensed a hint of irritation in our connection. "It is true, though. We can't go back. All we can do is move forward. That's all I want to do—move forward, lay this whole thing to rest. Stop my brother. Yilmaz. The lot of them."

"And we will," Cain said.

I sighed. "Well, if that's going to happen, we should head back to Dr. Ashter's office."

Cain agreed, and when we were almost there, I reached out and grabbed Cain's arm. "I remember."

Before he could respond, I turned and raced down the corridor.

31

And We're Off to the Races

I burst into Lio's office, Cain on my heels. "Get Miles up here now."

Lio didn't question me but sent the order. He looked at Cain, who shrugged.

"Ms. Orion? Care to fill me in?" Lio asked.

"Not until we're all here."

Soon, Miles slipped into Lio's office.

"Why was I summoned?" Miles asked.

"I know where I've seen those shapes and patterns before. Epo-5."

Miles looked horrified. "No. Please tell me I'm not going to have to wade through the waste bogs of that miserable little planet. I'll stink like a rotten fish for weeks."

I ignored him. "Yilmaz seized a letter Pops had left me with my lawyers. It was a thinly veiled attempt at a misdirection of where to go. I'm guessing he either didn't have much time to write it or something had happened. But that doesn't matter." I couldn't stand still, but the room wasn't big enough to pace, so I bounced on my heels a few times. "But he was referring to Epo-5. And I remember the glyph work from there. The patterns are similar. I'm sure of it."

Lio typed a few commands into his console, and the screen behind him lit up with reports and images from Epo-5.

"Now, bring up my files," I said.

He did, and I grinned.

"Not perfect matches, but they're similar. I bet if we had Sam run the patterns from my file through a database of images from Epo-5, we would find matches."

"And so, what are you saying? The Third is from Epo-5? That was the long-lost culture there?" Miles asked.

I shook my head. "No. I don't think the Third needs buildings or structures like what they've excavated on the planet." I threw a glance at Cain.

<*I agree,*> he thought.

"But I think whatever culture was there, knew about or had contact with the Third."

Lio turned back and stared at me. "I think it's time you filled me in on this Third."

So I did—on everything except the ship. I didn't want to share knowledge about that kind of tech, not yet. I trusted Lio, but I no longer trusted the system. Information had a way of finding itself in the wrong hands.

"You're confident this is where we need to go?" Lio asked after I finished debriefing him.

"Yes. And I need Sam to work on sorting and compiling everything we know about the planet. I believe these patterns are communication. I know research has been done before, but no one has ever come up with a solid linguistic pattern. But maybe I can help with that."

"What about Yilmaz?" Cain asked softly. "And Dr. Ashter? I assume this is what he's put together."

"I do too. That's why we're going to have to get there as fast as we can. And we're going to have to be prepared to fight."

The others all shared looks, and I understood. I was asking a lot—too much, probably. The IGJ had legions of ships they could call upon. I didn't know what Miles had or what resources Lio could produce.

"Look, I know this is where I need to go. We can't let Ashter or Yilmaz gain the upper hand. And we've got what they don't."

"And what's that?" Miles asked.

"Me." Then I filled Miles and Lio in on the strange visions I'd had.

Miles whistled. "So that's what they wanted. Their request to meet with you was the first time I've directly communicated with them. I knew that since they reached out to me, it was of the utmost importance."

"That doesn't explain what you did to the smart-bots," I said. "Yilmaz told me they'd been modified."

Miles shrugged, a sheepish look on his face. "That wasn't me."

Cain snarled, "Then who?"

"The Star Eaters. They sent them to me, along with their request."

"What?" I said. "You injected me with those things and you didn't know what they were?"

When Cain moved toward Miles, he raised his hands in defense. "Don't start with me," Miles said. "I'd been rooting around, trying to figure stuff out for years. I wasn't going to waste an opportunity like this when it landed in my lap."

"You're lucky I don't harbor more feelings of animosity than I do toward you," I snapped.

"Tell me what this means, exactly," Lio interjected.

I sighed. "It means we still don't know much. Other than my father worked with the Star Eaters at some point, they're tied up with the Third, and all roads are now leading to Epo-5."

"And that the Star Eaters or the Third, or both, are asking for your help," Cain said.

I nodded. "And I'll keep my promise."

Lio leaned back. "This is a lot of information to take in. I'll give navigation the orders to plot a course to Epo-5. But it might take longer than you want. We'll have to bypass any major areas or patrol points. And we need parts. The overdrive engine can function, but if we don't want to risk blowing ourselves up, we need to find a port to have some major work done."

Miles and Lio discussed a few options as I leaned back and considered everything. I wondered what my father had found on Epo-5 that made him send me a cryptic letter, enticing me to return.

As my mind shifted through several ideas and more questions, Cain turned and gave me a sharp look. "No."

Lio and Miles stopped their discussion and turned to look at us.

"It makes sense though, as much as I hate it," I said.

"We don't need to cross that line. Not yet," Cain said.

"One of you care to fill us in?" Miles asked.

I looked at him and grinned.

He frowned. "I don't like that look. What?"

"I need you to do something, and you're not going to like it. One bit."

But before I filled Miles in, I turned to Lio. "Let Cain and I have a shuttle. We'll head off to Epo-5. A small shuttle will draw far less attention, and we can skirt the major zones. You take the *Samaritan*, get her fixed up. Oh… one more thing. Sorry. I know this is a lot. But I need you to pick up the master."

"The who?" Miles asked.

"A Glipglow master who helped us out on the *Rapscallion*. I thought you knew everything."

Miles stuck his tongue out at me.

"Regardless, I asked him for some help on the smartbots, and he said he needed to see me in person. Even though it appears the Third took care of them, I want to know what he's worked on. Plus, when it comes to this level of biological tech, the master is exactly who we need. He might even be able to provide some insights into the Third."

"I'll work on that," Lio said. "I've still got some friends in high places who might help mask overdrive waste trails. And I'm sure we can meet up with this master when we get repairs taken care of. And…" He looked at me then at Cain. "If you're sure, I'll make sure you get the best shuttle we've got, plus a few members of the crew."

I opened my mouth to protest.

"No. That's not up for negotiation. You'll need help, and a few more eyes and ears won't hurt. We'll start working on supplies. Make a list of any gear you'll need for Epo-5."

"And so what about me?" Miles asked.

I turned and stared at him. "You're going to find the Star Eaters and bring them to Epo-5."

"Excuse me?" Miles said. "What makes you think I'm going to do that? Or that I even can?"

"Come on. You've got connections everywhere. Besides, something tells me they're going to be easy to find this time."

I threw a look at Cain, who was decidedly unhappy, his tail snapping back and forth.

"They knew Pops, they saved me on the *Rapscallion*, they wanted me infected with smart-bots they modified. We need to talk to them."

Miles mumbled a few things I didn't catch, but his shoulders slumped forward. "Fine. I'll see what I can do. But I'm not making any promises, mind you."

"Drop my name, then, if you need to. They're obviously invested in me."

Cain finally spoke up. "You don't know that. What if they forced your father? Or worse?"

"No. I don't think so."

"And what about Lucas?" Lio asked.

"I don't know," I honestly replied. "I have no intention of meeting with him, at least not until I figure out all these bizarre connections. He's too dangerous not to be armed when I have to deal with him."

<What if Lucas has already figured it out? What if the tech he's using to destroy worlds is what everyone is after?>

I stiffened. That was possible. We'd seen what the Third could do, how it had destroyed that area of Dar. *<If that's the case, then we need to understand it too. And this is how we do it. I need to know what's special about Epo-5.>*

<Alright. Then that's what we do.>

I leaned back and let them hash out the plans, my mind at peace with our course of action. I didn't know what was going to happen or if we'd even be able to connect the dots, let alone stop Lucas.

But maybe I would at least figure out what had forced my father to do what he'd done. At least I would get some closure there.

Cain looked at me, concern in his violet eyes. I gave him a soft smile. *<I'm okay.>*

And that was true. The worlds might've been falling into chaos around us, and the journey ahead of us looked bleak, but for the first time in a long time, I felt a sense of peace within myself.

I was Mahia Orion. And I was going to unravel the mysteries of Epo-5.

Thank you for reading *The Diplomats of Dar*!

Don't miss out on what happens next for Mahia and Cain or explore what other titles I have to offer. You can sign-up to stay in touch through my newsletter at:

elizabethknollston.com

You can also follow me on social media at:
facebook.com/elizabethknollston
twitter.com/EKnollston

Look for the fourth installment of the
The Three-Fold Suns Series

The Secrets of Epo-5

and discover the twists and turns that are on the horizon!

Acknowledgements

Looking at the world and the universe beyond with questioning eyes and a curious mind was because of the encouragement I received from my parents. Without their love and support, this journey of becoming an author wouldn't have been possible. I will forever cherish the memories of adventurous vacations, the love of reading, and the support of being who I am.

I've been fortunate to find so many others along this journey to share my love of imagination and far-flung worlds. Being able to surround myself with people who have cheered me on to write and share the stories I create has been a wonderful gift of friendship and found family.

All I can say is an endless string of deep and grateful thank yous to everyone who has helped and supported me along the way.

And without the wonderful editors at Red Adept Editing, this story wouldn't be where it is today without all of their hard work to push me and help polish this story! Thank you so much for all that you have done.

Thank you to all of my readers for your interest in my work and believing in me! I am so grateful for your taking a chance on this book and leaving your kind words of reviews and encouragement. And I look forward to writing more far-flung adventures to share with you all!

About the Author

Elizabeth Knollston collects dragons. No, they're not real. But if you know of a mad scientist or genetic engineer who's working on the real deal, be sure to let her know. She would dearly love to collect star ships too, but those won't fit in her garage.

Her (overactive) imagination is credit to her parents, who outrageously encouraged her poor spending habits of buying too many books. And just a side note—if you ever plan on moving, book collecting isn't helpful.

In another life, Elizabeth dreamed of becoming an archaeologist, but a fascinating and rewarding job as a therapeutic horseback riding instructor derailed those plans. When Elizabeth isn't wondering about being on a manned mission to Mars, she enjoys bugging her dog, battling the weeds in her garden, and being a productive member of society.

Made in the USA
Columbia, SC
05 October 2023